THE WEDDING CAKE IN THE MIDDLE OF THE ROAD

23 VARIATIONS ON A THEME

W·W·NORTON & COMPANY · NEW YORK · LONDON

THE WEDDING CAKE IN THE MIDDLE OF THE ROAD

EDITED BY Susan Stamberg
AND George Garrett

The text of this book is composed in Electra, with the display type set in
Bernhard Modern. Composition by PennSet. Manufacturing by
The Haddon Craftsmen, Inc.
Book design by Antonina Krass.

Library of Congress Cataloging in Publication Data
The Wedding cake in the middle of the road : 23 variations on a theme
/ edited and with introductions by Susan Stamberg
and George Garrett.
    p.   cm.
    1. Short stories, American.   I. Stamberg, Susan
II. Garrett, George
PS648.S5W43   1992
813'.0108–dc20   91-16273

ISBN 0–393–03080–6

W. W. Norton & Company, Inc., 500 Fifth Avenue, New York, N. Y. 10110
W. W. Norton & Company, Ltd., 10 Coptic Street, London WC1A 1PU

1 2 3 4 5 6 7 8 9 0

For our spouses:

. . . Susan Garrett, who once bought a wedding dress in Filene's basement for $11.
. . . Louis Stamberg, who knew enough to eat the roses.

Contents

Introduction I

SUSAN STAMBERG

This book began with a radio program. Not such an unlikely genesis. Radio plays music, gives weather, follows sports, delivers news. But radio is most powerful when it tells stories. Maybe it has something to do with the mother's voice—that first storyteller in our lives. Or, more primal, the hunters' tales, around the fire, when prehistory was written in the smudge of palms on cave walls. Anyway, storytelling is radio's art; tales told on the air as compelling, often, as those on the printed page.

In 1987 we were creating a new National Public Radio program. As host, I wanted to include writing, storytelling. My reasons were purely personal. The program aired on Sunday mornings—the most stay-at-home time of the week. To me, staying home with the radio meant staying home with a roomful of fabulous visitors. In the radio days of my childhood I loved nothing more than being home with a head cold and having the stories of *Stella Dallas* or *Our Gal Sunday* spin out just for me, from the little box on the kitchen table. Those visits—those storytelling visitors—were so addictive I almost hated getting better. Nothing in second or fifth grade could have been as remotely compelling as the dilemmas of Stella's daughter Lollie or the adventures of an orphan girl from a small mining town in the West. I absorbed their stories in the kitchen over bowls of steaming chicken soup or in bed (the radio moved to my room, a very special concession), propped up with extra pillows, nose drops and tissues at hand. My mother—my first storyteller, with her lilting voice and her flair for reading aloud—presided over the sickroom, heating soup, plumping the pillows, enjoying with me the soap opera stories. Somehow, being cared for and cared about got caught up with stories on the radio. So when the time came to do radio myself, I knew storytelling had to be part of it.

Weekend Edition's first Sunday broadcast included Chapter One of what I believe is the first radio equivalent of the chain novel. It was soap-opera-like in inspiration. Each Sunday we presented a new chapter, written and read aloud by a different author. A kind of literary relay race, it was a way to get good writing on the air, satisfy my storytelling predilections, and build an audience for a new program. The chain novel created continuity. Listeners tuned in week after week to hear the story unfold. David Leavitt wrote the first chapter, and the literary baton was passed, most hilariously and circuitously, to, among others, Russell Banks, Richard Bausch (you'll notice that he and David Leavitt are also in this collection), Lorrie Moore, Stanley Elkin, Meg and Hilma Wolitzer.

After the chain novel came a chain mystery (Gregory Mcdonald, in this volume, took part in that one). Again, an exercise in literary fellowship. Sixteen different writers, including Tony Hillerman, Mary Higgins Clark, and Donald E. Westlake, amplified or completely sandbagged one another's plot lines and characters Sunday morning after Sunday morning.

The chain books were fun, and wonderfully written. They kept listeners near the radio. But they weren't exactly belles-lettres. Too many bumps in the plots, too many different voices. Then Stacey Freed, a young student of creative writing at George Mason University who'd been following our various literary capers on *Weekend Edition* Sunday, suggested that instead of asking a group of writers to link together a single long story, we should give them the same image and ask each to do a separate, very short story, based on the image.

A cake, a wedding cake, was our starting point. And not just any wedding cake. Location was important. This was a wedding cake in the middle of the road. George Garrett chose the image itself. A few pages from now he will describe its origin and his own history with a similar literary exercise. Garrett's singular roadside attraction was presented to six writers along with an invitation to work with it, for radio. The assignment was no piece of cake: write two and a half pages (all right, four if you insist), typewritten, double-spaced, a complete short story, incorporating that strangely perched cake. The image is distinctive. It's vivid. We asked the six authors to take it somewhere for us, please. See what it attached itself to, in their imaginations.

To me, it's a funny picture. I envisioned the cake falling off the back of a pickup truck en route to a ceremony in Thonotosassa, Florida. No one did that. To Judith Guest, it was a sad image; she produced an old-fashioned love story around it. Joy Williams made the wedding cake the basis of a Doomsday scenario. Of the rest of the original six who wrote for radio, Ann Beattie had a cake without a wedding, Ron Carlson looked back

on a twenty-year marriage, George Garrett found a new relationship shadowed by divorce, and Stuart Dybek created an entire
coming-of-age novel in three and a half pages. Their stories are
scattered throughout this collection, in the same short form in
which they were written for broadcast.

And here too, off the air, are stories solicited expressly for this
book from a range of writers of varying ages, backgrounds, and
literary bents. With great good nature and commendable gen-
erosity, these authors agreed to participate in this literary exercise.
Their replies—RSVPs that run from three to twenty-one pages
—take the cake in many directions.

Bringing the gifts of their story-making, a total of twenty-three
writers, from the best-known to the brand-new, come up with a
breathtaking range of responses. Each one is distinctive, fully
realized, rich in voice and characterization.

A disproportionate number of Southerners populate these
pages. Possibly because Southerners are so good at telling stories.
In the South, the untruth is less a sin than an opportunity for
fabulism. "Storying" there is what we Northerners call, less gracefully, lying. But surely the best writers are the most glorious
fabricators. It's one of the things that separates them from jour-
nalists.

The anthology is, finally, a testimonial to the literary imagination. In addition to being a gathering of marvelous stories, the
collection is, implicitly, about how the imagination works and
how it can work, in its infinite variety. As these authors stretch
their talents around the same central image, and are inspired by
it to such various ends, they remind us of why storytelling has
always been so compelling, whether written or spoken.

The radio connection remains for some of the original writers,
possibly because they were writing for the medium, possibly because it had transfixed them, once, as it has me. "Calla lilies

look like microphones" on the cake in Ann Beattie's story. Stuart Dybek's young protagonist says of Trish, the wedding-cake bride who brings such magic to her husband's life, that "the most beautiful songs on the radio came after she turned it on."

Perhaps this printed anthology keeps the songs coming.

Introduction II

GEORGE GARRETT

In the beginning was the girl in the black raincoat. Now that was long ago in the early 1960s at Mr. Jefferson's university in Virginia, a place which had not yet seen the light or seen fit to admit young women, coeds, to its lawn and grounds, its halls and colonnades. All that would change soon enough, and high time, too; but then there were only a few young women who, for one complicated reason or exception, were being permitted to study at the university. One of these, over from Mary Washington, where she couldn't find the advanced philosophy courses she needed, was Kelly Cherry. Kelly came to my creative writing class, shy and soft-voiced and gifted and quite beautiful, and

more than a little mysterious in the long black buttoned-up raincoat she wore always and everywhere, its hem barely revealing
the blue sneakers she also always had on. Long before punk, her
hair was an extravagantly artificial red. And, needless to say, all
of the young men in my class those days, still coat-and-tie days
(though some of them affected early signs of rebellion from dress
codes and other authoritarian impositions by going barefoot or,
anyway, without socks), all of them were madly, possessively,
irrepressibly in love with her. So was I, I reckon, a little. So was
everybody.

One day for some reason she dropped out of the university.
Was gone out of our lives for good and all, it seemed. In her
absence a student in the class, Henry Taylor, a poet who one
day would win for himself the Pulitzer Prize, wrote a story about
her called, as I recall, "And Bid a Fond Farewell to Tennessee."
As was the custom of that class, he read the story aloud and then,
as it happened, took any amount of loud and vociferous criticism,
flak really, from all the other students in the class. They easily
recognized Kelly as the "Tennessee" in his story and clearly
resented his fictional claim to her life and times. Jealousy, no
matter how pure, is an awkward argument; so the voiced com-
plaint was that you should never use "real" people and events in
fiction. Pedagogically the answer to all this was the requirement
that *everybody* in class should go and write something about a
girl in a black raincoat. The idea was, of course, to let them
learn by doing some of the ways and means by which fiction can
shape and transform the factually "real" into something else,
another kind of truth.

That might have been that, the end of it, except that there
were a couple of writers visiting Virginia at the time, who,
hearing about the exercise and intrigued by the evocative pos-

sibilities of the image, joined in. Soon, without plan and organization or serious intention, manuscripts of stories and poems about girls in black raincoats began to come to me. As if I had some plan or idea what to do with them. Eventually, thanks to the adventurous interest of an old-fashioned publisher, the late Charles Duell of Duell, Sloan & Pearce, there was a book, composed of some of this material and including, by editorial design and in almost equal proportion, fine professional writers (some already well known, some soon to be) as well as beginners. Among the latter, Kelly Cherry herself. And Henry Taylor and Annie Dillard and others. Among the former were folks like Leslie Fiedler and Shelby Foote, May Sarton and Mary Lee Settle, William Jay Smith and Donald Justice and Mark Strand.

The Girl in the Black Raincoat appeared in 1965 and was very widely reviewed; and the best part of all that unanticipated attention was that sooner or later, each and every single contributor to the book was declared by some critic or reviewer somewhere or other to be the creator of the best thing in the whole book. No matter how they felt about the work itself (reception was mixed and a good many of the big-time people in the big-time places felt it was all a little too frivolous), reviewers always found something worthy of notice and admiration; and I could send a clipping to the contributor.

Cut directly to 1989 and the next phase. Which Susan has already described and which calls for only a few more words from me. Once Susan had challenged me to come up with another image, one which might possibly arouse the interest, imaginations, and energies of other writers in somewhat the same way that the black raincoat had, all this for a "literary game" on *Weekend Edition*, I found myself looking, weighing and sifting, waiting in ambush for something to come along. What came along pretty soon was a story by a talented young woman, a student of mine named Beverly Goodrum. One element in her story, not absolutely essential to it at that stage, but nonetheless surprising and evocative in context, was the vision by the protagonist of a wedding cake (real or imaginary) sitting there all by itself in a median strip, the big middle of a busy freeway. Beverly's flaky central character flashed by at high speed and couldn't believe her eyes or trust her memory. I couldn't believe mine either. It looked like we had our image. And we did.

We also have Beverly Goodrum's story, changed and developed now, to be sure, out of which the image came.

There are some connections with the old *Girl in the Black Raincoat*. It's all stories this time, no poems on board; but Kelly Cherry is appropriately included. And Mary Lee Settle, as artistically alive and adventurous as she was then, has created a wedding cake story for the book. There are some newcomers, too, as before. In addition to Beverly Goodrum, here is Brian Klam, with his first published story. He wrote it, first of all, as a class exercise for his workshop with Madison Smartt Bell. Here also is Hannah Wilson, who heard the stories on the radio and sent her own to Susan Stamberg simply to respond to the program in kind. So, as in *Raincoat*, there's some honorable "discovery" going on here.

You don't have to be a literary critic—it helps *not* to be one —to see that even though all these stories share the image of a wedding cake in the middle of the road, and some of them share, inevitably, some minor details, no two of them are really much alike. The six that were originally broadcast on National Public Radio are of a certain size and length (style, too)—short because they had to be. The other stories are of various lengths, but none seems to be long-winded.

Different as they are from each other, all the stories in this gathering have something more, something deeper, than the central image in common. They each and all, to one degree and another, exemplify the spirit of play, of *free play*, which is at the heart and soul of so much art. *Homo ludens.* We are playful creatures even at our most serious moments. Without play, our little plays, we would be swept away without a trace. Without play, the world that comes at us every day would all be too terrible and serious to bear. The playful visions and versions of truth to be found here, even the bleakest of them (and some are pretty bleak), are celebrations of another kind of wedding, the mystical marriage of spirit and flesh, of art and life, of Creation and the creatures in and of it, and, yes, too, of writer and reader.

Lest we end on too high and extravagant a note for what is supposed to be an entertaining anthology of new fiction, let me, not without pride, remind the imaginary reader of something special about this book. (The same thing was special in *The Girl in the Black Raincoat.*) The making of anthologies is a busy little industry. And there are all kinds of anthologies, many of them built around a common subject or region or theme. These are almost always culled from existing, published material. The connection, unity if you will, is at once editorial and accidental. Here, in two stages, first for *Weekend Edition* and then for this book, all the material was consciously and deliberately created by the writers for the occasion. They did not work together, of course. Indeed, most of them had little idea who else was also involved. But they made something to be part of and to fit into something larger.

None of this means that this collection is better (or worse) than any other, more conventionally made anthology. But it does mean that this gathering of stories is different, and its very difference demonstrates the power of creativity. Long live the difference.

Acknowledgments

Thanks to the staff of *Weekend Edition* Sunday, past and present, especially Katherine Ferguson, our first producer; Chris Buchanan and Andy Bowers, who dealt with the first made-for-broadcast writings; and Connie Drummer, who handled the daunting paperwork. Joni Markovitz donated her marvelous organizational skills to the wedding cake project and its radio mystery predecessor. Alan Cheuse was generous, as always, with suggestions of authors to include. Ronni Krasnow and Carey Suleiman helped with various aspects of this book.

And thanks to all the writers for playing the game.

THE WEDDING CAKE IN THE MIDDLE OF THE ROAD

I Never Told This to Anyone

STUART DYBEK

I never told this to anyone—there wasn't anyone to tell it to—but when I was living with my Uncle Kirby on the Edge—the edge of what I never knew for sure ("Just livin' on the Edge, don't worry *where*," Uncle Kirby would say)—a little bride and groom would come to visit me at night. Naturally, I never mentioned this to Uncle Kirby. He'd have acted like I was playing with dolls. "A boy should play like the wild animals do—to practice survival," Uncle Kirby always said. "You wanna play, play with your Uzi."

The bride wore a white gown and silver slippers, and held a bouquet. The groom wore top hat, tails, and spats. Their shoes were covered with frosting as if they'd walked through snow even though it was summer, June, when they first appeared. I heard a little pop—actually, more of a *pip!*—and there on my windowsill was the groom, pouring from a tiny champagne bottle. "Hi! I'm Jay and this is Trish," he said by way of introduction, adding almost confidentially, "We don't think of one another as Mr. and Mrs. yet."

They had tiny voices, but I could hear them clearly. "That's because we enunciate," Trish said. She was pretty.

"It's these formal clothes, Old Boy," Jay explained. "Put them on and you start to speak the King's English."

I remember the first night they appeared, and the nights that followed, as celebrations—like New Year's Eve in June. There'd be big-band music on my short wave—a station I could never locate except when Jay and Trish were over—and the *pip! pip! pip!* of miniature champagne bottles. You should have seen them dancing to "Out of Nowhere" in the spotlight my flashlight threw as it followed them across the floor. I'd applaud and Jay would kiss the bride. But each celebration seemed as if it would be the last.

"Off for the honeymoon, Old Boy," Jay would always say with a wink as they left. He'd sweep Trish off her feet and carry her across the windowsill, and Trish would laugh and wave back at me, "*Ciao*—we'll be staying at the Motel d'Amore," and then she'd toss her small bouquet.

I didn't want them to go. Having their visits to look forward to made living on the Edge seem less desolate. Uncle Kirby noticed the change in me. "What's with *You*, lately," he asked —*You* was sort of his nickname for me. "I mean, why *You* goin' round with rice in your pockets and wearin' that jazzbow tie? And what's with the old shoes and tin cans tied to the back fender a your bike? How *You* expect to survive that way when the next attack comes outa nowhere?"

I told him that dragging shoes and cans built up my endurance and the rice was emergency rations, and he left me alone, but I knew he was keeping an eye on me.

Luckily, no matter how often Jay and Trish said they were off, they'd show up again a few nights later, back on the windowsill, scraping the frosting from their shoes. And after a while, when they'd leave, walking away hand in hand into the shadows, Jay hooking his tux jacket over his shoulder rather than sweeping Trish off her feet, and Trish no longer carrying a bouquet to toss, neither of them would mention the honeymoon.

I didn't notice at first, but gradually the nights quieted down. "A little more sedate an evening for a change," Jay would say. Trish, especially, seemed quieter. She said that champagne had begun making her dizzy. After dancing, she'd need a nap.

"I get no kick from champagne," Jay would tell her, raising his glass in a toast, "but I get a kick out of you."

Trish would smile back, blow him a kiss, and then close her eyes. While she rested, Jay would sit up and talk to me. He had a confidential way of speaking that made it seem as if he was always on the verge of revealing a secret, as if we shared the closeness of conspirators.

"Actually," he'd say, almost whispering, "I still *do* get a kick from champagne, although it's nothing compared to what I feel around Trish. I never told this to anyone, but I married her simply because she brought magic into my life. The most beautiful songs on the radio came after she turned it on. She made my routine, ordinary life seem somehow magical."

It wasn't until the sweltering nights of late summer, when Jay and Trish began to bicker and argue, that I realized how much things had changed. The two of them even looked different, larger somehow, as if they were outgrowing their now stained, shabby formal wear.

"I'm so tired of this ratty dress," Trish complained one evening.

"Now it's nag nag nag instead of *pip pip pip*," Jay replied.
"And please don't say *ratty*. You know how I despise the term."

Jay would harangue us on the subject of rodents in a way that reminded me of Uncle Kirby on the subject of Commies or certain ethnic groups. Jay had developed a bit of a potbelly and looked almost as if he was copying Trish, who was, by now, obviously expecting. "Expecting" was Trish's word. "Out of all the names they give it, Old Boy, don't you think 'expecting' sounds the prettiest?" she'd asked me once, surprising me, and I quickly agreed.

Their visits had become regular, and they showed up, increasingly ravenous, to dine on the morsels I'd filched from the supper table at Jay's suggestion. "Old Boy," Jay had said, jokingly, "you can't just take the attitude of 'Let them eat cake.' After all, cake isn't a limitless resource, you know." I was glad to pilfer the food for them. It made mealtime an adventure. Stealing rations in front of Uncle Kirby wasn't easy.

After I served their little dinner, they'd stay and visit. Jay would sit drinking the beer he'd figured a way of siphoning from Uncle Kirby's home brew.

"We could use a goddam TV around this godforsaken, boring place. It would be nice to watch a little bowling once in a while," Jay would gripe after he'd had a few too many.

"Maybe if you'd do something besides sitting around in your dirty underwear, drinking and belching, things wouldn't be so BORrrr-ing," Trish answered.

Once, after an argument that made Trish storm off in tears, Jay held his head and muttered, as if more to himself than to me, "I never told this to anyone, but me and the Mrs. *had* to get married."

By the time the leaves were falling, they'd shed their wedding clothes. Trish wore a dress cut from one of my sweat socks, boots of bumblebee fur, and a hat made from a hummingbird's nest. Jay, bearded, a blue jay feather poking from his top hat, dressed in the gray skin of an animal he refused to identify. He carried a knitting-needle spear, a bow he'd fashioned from the wishbone of a turkey, and a quiver of arrows—disposable hypodermic needles he'd scavenged from Uncle Kirby's supplies. He tipped each arrow in cottonmouth venom.

They never appeared now without first scavenging Uncle Kirby's storehoused supplies—at least, they called it scavenging. Uncle Kirby called it guerrilla warfare. He kept scrupulous inventories of his stockpiles, and detected, almost immediately, even the slightest invasion. Yet no matter how carefully he protected his supplies, Jay found ways to infiltrate his defenses. Jay avoided poisons, raided traps, short-circuited alarms, picked locks, solved combinations, and carried off increasing amounts of Uncle Kirby's stuff. Even more than the loss of supplies, Jay's boldness and cleverness began to obsess Uncle Kirby.

"Hey, *You*," Uncle Kirby told me. "You're about to witness something you'll remember the resta your life—short as that might be, given the way you're goin' at it. Kirby Versus the Varmints!"

It was the season to worry about supplies, to calculate the caches of food and jerry cans of water, the drums of fuel oil surrounded by barbed wire, the cords of scrap wood. Each night the wind honed its edge sharper in the bare branches. Each night came earlier. Lit by the flicker of my kerosene stove, Jay plucked the turkey bow as if it were an ancient single-stringed instrument. He played in accompaniment to the wind and to Trish's plaintive singing—an old folk song, she said, called "Expectations." The wind and the wandering melody reminded me of the sound of the ghostly frequencies on my shortwave. The ghostly frequencies were the only stations I could pick up anymore, except for a station from far north on the dial that sounded as if it was broadcasting crows.

"Listen," Jay said, amused, "they're giving the crow financial report: 'Tuck away a little nest egg.' "

While we huddled around the stove, listening to the newscast of crows, Uncle Kirby was in his workshop, working late over an endless series of traps, baited cages, zappers. He invented the KBM (Kirby Better Mousetrap), the KRS (Kirby Rodent Surprise), and the KSPG (Kirby Small Pest Guillotine), which worked well enough in testing to cost him the tip of his little finger. Some of these inventions actually worked on rodents, and Uncle Kirby took to displaying his trophies by their tails. He devised trip wires, heat sensors, and surveillance monitors, but when Jay's raids continued despite Uncle Kirby's best efforts, the exhilaration of combat turned nasty. We were sitting at the supper table one evening over Kirby Deluxe—leftover meat loaf dipped in batter and deep-fried—and I'd stashed a couple bites along with a few canned peas away for Jay and Trish when Uncle Kirby suddenly said, "All right, *You*, what's with the food in your cuffs?"

I tried to think of some reason he might believe, and realized we were beyond that, so I just hung my head over my plate.

"Look, *You*," Uncle Kirby said, shaking his bandaged hand in my face, "there's something mysterious going on here. I don't know what little game you're playin', but I think a preemptive strike's in order."

He left me trussed to a kitchen chair, and that night he handcuffed my ankle to the bunk. It was the night of the first snow. Jay appeared late, kicking the snow from his moleskin boots.

"Trish asked me to say goodbye for her, Old Boy," Jay said. "It's getting a bit barbarous around here, you know."

I turned my face to the wall.

"She said to tell you that she wants to name the baby after

you, unless it's a girl, of course, in which case 'Old Boy' wouldn't be appropriate."

I didn't laugh. When you're trying to hold back tears, laughing can suddenly make you cry.

"This isn't like us going off on a honeymoon, Old Boy," Jay said. He was busy picking the lock on the handcuffs with his knitting-needle spear. "We never did get to the Motel d'Amore, but that time we spent here in summer, that *was* the honeymoon. I never told this to anyone, but maybe someday you'll understand, if you're lucky enough to meet someone who'll make you feel as if your heart is wearing a tuxedo, as if your soul is standing in a chapel in the moonlight and your life is rushing like a limo running red lights, you'll understand how one day you open your eyes and it's as if you find yourself standing on top of a wedding cake in the middle of the road, an empty highway, without a clue as to how you got there, but then, that's all part of coming out of nowhere, isn't it?"

When they didn't return the next night, I knew I'd never see them again, and I picked the lock as I'd seen Jay do with the knitting needle he'd left behind, and cut the cans and shoes off my bike and took off, too. It wasn't easy. Uncle Kirby had booby-trapped the perimeter. I knew he'd come looking for me, that, for him, finding me would seem like something out of the only story he'd ever read me—"The Most Dangerous Game." But I knew about my own secret highway—I never told this to anyone—a crumbling strip of asphalt, a shadow of an old two-lane, overgrown, no more of it left than a peeling center stripe through a swamp. I rode that center stripe as if balanced on the edge of a blade. It took me all the way to here.

Tandolfo the Great

RICHARD BAUSCH

"Tandolfo," he says to his own image in the mirror over the bathroom sink. "She loves you not, you goddam fool."

He's put the makeup on, packed the bag of tricks—including the rabbit, whom he calls Chi-Chi; and the bird, the attention-getter, which he calls Witch. He's to do a birthday party on the other side of the river. Some five-year-old, and so this is going to be one of those tough ones, a crowd of babies, and all the adults waiting around for him to screw up.

He has fortified himself with something, and he feels ready. He isn't particularly worried about it. But there's a little something else he has to do first. Something on the order of the embarrassingly ridiculous: he has to make a small delivery.

This morning, at the local bakery, he picked up a big pink

wedding cake, with its six tiers and its scalloped edges and its little bride and groom on top. He'd ordered it on his own; he'd taken the initiative, planning to offer it to a young woman of his acquaintance. He managed somehow to set the thing on the backseat of the car and when he got home he found a note from her announcing, all excited and happy, that she's engaged. The man she'd had such trouble with has had a change of heart; he wants to get married after all. She's going to Houston to live. She loves her dear old Tandolfo with a big kiss and a hug always, and she knows he'll have every happiness. She's so thankful for his friendship. Her magic man. He's her sweet clown. She has actually driven over here and, finding him gone, left the note for him, folded under the door knocker—her pink notepaper, with the little tangle of flowers at the top. She wants him to call her, come by as soon as he can to help celebrate. *Please*, she says. *I want to give you a big hug.* He read this and then walked out to stand on the sidewalk and look at the cake in its place on the backseat of the car.

"Good God," he said.

He'd thought he would put the clown outfit on, deliver the cake in person in the evening; an elaborate proposal to a girl he's never even kissed. He's a little unbalanced, and he knows it. Over the months of their working together for the county government, he's built up tremendous feelings of loyalty and yearning toward her. He thought she felt something, too. He interpreted gestures—her hand lingering on his shoulder when he made her laugh; her endearments to him, tinged as they seemed to be with a kind of sadness, as if she were afraid for what the world might do to someone so romantic.

"You sweet clown," she said. And she said it a lot. And she talked to him about her ongoing trouble, the guy she'd been in love with who kept waffling about getting married. He wanted no commitments. Tandolfo, aka Rodney Wilbury, told her that he hated men who weren't willing to run the risks of love. Why, he personally was the type who'd always believed in marriage and children, lifelong commitments. He had caused difficulties for himself and life was a disappointment so far, but he believed in falling in love and starting a family. She didn't hear him. It all went right through her like white noise on the radio. For weeks he had come around to visit her, had invited her to watch him perform. She confided in him, and he thought of movies where the friend sticks around and is a good listener, and eventually gets the girl. They fall in love. He put his hope in that. He was optimistic; he'd ordered and bought the cake. Apparently the whole time, all through the listening and being noble with her, she thought of it as nothing more than friendship, accepting it from him because she was accustomed to being offered friendship.

Now he leans close to the mirror to look at his own eyes through the makeup. They look clear enough. "Loves you absolutely not. You must be crazy. You must be the great Tandolfo."

Yes.

Twenty-six-year-old, out-of-luck Tandolfo. In love. With a great oversized cake in the backseat of his car. It's Sunday, a cool April day. He's a little inebriated. That's the word he prefers. It's polite; it suggests something faintly silly. Nothing could be sillier than to be dressed like this in the broad daylight, and to go driving across the bridge into Virginia to put on a magic show. Nothing could be sillier than to have spent all that money on a completely useless purchase—a cake six tiers high. Maybe fifteen pounds of sugar.

When he has made his last check of the clown face in the mirror, and the bag of tricks and props, he goes to his front door and stands at the screen looking out at the architectural shadow of it in the backseat. The inside of the car will smell like icing for days. He'll have to keep the windows open even if it rains; he'll go to work smelling like confectionery delights. The whole thing makes him laugh. A wedding cake. He steps out of the house and makes his way in the late-afternoon sun down the sidewalk to the car. As if they have been waiting for him, three boys come skating down from the top of the hill. He has the feeling that if he tried to sneak out like this at two in the morning, someone would come by and see him anyway. "Hey, Rodney," one boy says. "I mean Tandolfo."

Tandolfo recognizes him. A neighborhood boy, a tough. Just the kind to make trouble, just the kind with no sensitivity to the suffering of others. "Leave me alone or I'll turn you into spaghetti," he says.

"Hey, guys—it's Tandolfo the Great." The boy's hair is a bright blond color, and you can see through it to his scalp.

"Scram," Tandolfo says. "Really."

"Aw, what's your hurry, man?"

"I've just set off a nuclear device," Tandolfo says with grave seriousness. "It's on a timer. Poof."

"Do a trick for us," the blond one says. "Where's that scurvy rabbit of yours?"

"I gave it the week off." Someone, last winter, poisoned the first Chi-Chi. He keeps the cage indoors now. "I'm in a hurry. No rabbit to help with the driving."

But they're interested in the cake now. "Hey, what's that in your car? Is that what I think it is?"

"Just stay back."

"Is that a cake, man? Is that real?"

Tandolfo gets his cases into the trunk, and hurries to the driver's side door. The three boys are peering into the backseat.

"Hey, man. A cake. Can we have a piece of cake?"

"Back off," Tandolfo says.

The white-haired one says, "Come on, Tandolfo."

"Hey, Tandolfo, I saw some guys looking for you, man. They said you owed them money."

He gets in, ignoring them. He starts the car.

"You sucker," one of them says.

"Hey, man. Who's the cake for?"

He drives away, thinks of himself leaving them in a cloud of exhaust. Riding through the green shade, he glances in the rear-view mirror and sees the clown face, the painted smile. It makes him want to laugh. He tells himself he's his own cliché—a clown with a broken heart. Looming behind him is the cake, like a passenger in the backseat.

He drives slow. He has always believed viscerally that gestures mean everything. When he moves his hands and brings about the effects that amaze little children, he feels larger than life, unforgettable. He learned the magic while in high school, as a way of making friends, and though it didn't really make him any friends, he's been practicing it ever since. It's an extra source of income, and lately income has had a way of disappearing too quickly. He's been in some trouble—betting the horses; betting the sports events. He's hungover all the time. There have been several polite warnings at work. He's managed so far to tease everyone out of the serious looks, the cool evaluative study of his face. The fact is, people like him in an abstract way, the way they like distant clownish figures: the comedian whose name they can't remember. He can see it in their eyes. Even the rough characters after his loose change have a certain sense of humor about it. He's a phenomenon, a subject of conversation.

There's traffic on Key Bridge, and he's stuck for a while. It becomes clear that he'll have to go straight to the birthday party.

Sitting behind the wheel of the car with his cake on the backseat, he becomes aware of people in other cars noticing him. In the car to his left, a girl stares, chewing gum. She waves, rolls her window down. Two others are with her, one in the backseat. "Hey," she says. He nods. Smiles inside what he knows is the painted smile. His teeth will look dark against the makeup.

"Where's the party?" she says.

But the traffic moves again. He concentrates. The snarl is on the other side of the bridge—construction of some kind. He can see the cars lined up, waiting to go up the hill into Roslyn and beyond. Time is beginning to be a consideration. In his glove box he has a flask of bourbon. He reaches over and takes it out, looks around himself. No police anywhere. Just the idling cars and people tuning their radios or arguing or simply staring out as if at some distressing event. The smell of the cake is making him woozy. He takes a swallow of the bourbon, then puts it back. The car with the girls in it goes by him in the left lane, and they are not even looking at him. He watches them go on ahead. He's in the wrong lane again; he can't remember a time when *his* lane was the only one moving. He told her once that he considered himself in the race of people who gravitate to the nonmoving lanes of highways, and who cause traffic lights to turn yellow by approaching them. She took the idea and carried it out a little —saying she was of the race of people who emitted enzymes which instilled a sense of impending doom in marriageable young men, and made them wary of long-term relationships.

"No," Tandolfo/Rodney said. "I'm living proof that isn't so. I have no such fear, and I'm with you."

"But you're of the race of people who make mine relax all the enzymes."

"You're not emitting the enzymes now. I see."

"No," she said. "It's only with marriageable young men."

"I emit enzymes that prevent people like you from seeing that I'm a marriageable young man."

"I'm too relaxed to tell," she said, and touched his shoulder. A plain affectionate moment that gave him tossing nights and fever.

Because of the traffic, he arrives late at the birthday party. He gets out of the car and two men come down from the house to greet him. He keeps his face turned away, remembering too late the breath mints in his pocket.

"Jesus," one of the men says. "Look at this. Hey—who comes out of the cake? This is a kid's birthday party."

"The cake stays."

"What does he mean, it stays? Is that a trick?"

They're both looking at him. The one spoken to must be the birthday boy's father—he's wearing a party cap that says DAD. He has long dirty-looking strands of blond hair jutting out from the cap, and there are streaks of sweaty grit on the sides of his face. "So you're the Great Tandolfo," he says, extending a meaty red hand. "Isn't it hot in that makeup?"

"No, sir."

"We've been playing volleyball."

"You've exerted yourselves."

They look at him. "What do you do with the cake?" the one in the DAD cap asks.

"Cake's not part of the show, actually."

"You just carry it around with you?"

The other man laughs. He's wearing a T-shirt with a smile face on the chest. "This ought to be some show," he says.

They all make their way across the street and the lawn, to the porch of the house. It's a big party—bunting everywhere and children gathering quickly to see the clown.

"Ladies and gentlemen," says the man in the DAD cap. "I give you Tandolfo the Great."

Tandolfo isn't ready yet. He's got his cases open, but he needs a table to put everything on. The first trick is where he releases the bird. He'll finish with the best trick, in which the rabbit appears as if from a pan of flames: it always draws a gasp, even from the adults; the fire blooms in the pan, down goes the "lid"—it's the rabbit's tight container—the latch is tripped, and the skin of the "lid" lifts off. *Voilà!* Rabbit. The fire is put out by the fireproof cage bottom. He's gotten pretty good at making the switch, and if the crowd isn't too attentive—as children often are not—he can perform certain hand tricks with some style. But he needs a table, and he needs time to set up.

The whole crowd of children is seated in front of the door into the house. He's standing there on the porch, his back to the stairs, and he's been introduced.

"Hello, boys and girls," he says, and bows. "Tandolfo needs a table."

"A table," one of the women says. All the adults are ranged against the porch wall, behind the children. He sees light sweaters, shapely hips, and wild tresses; he sees beer cans in tight fists and heavy jowls, bright ice-blue eyes. A little row of faces, and one elderly face. He feels more inebriated than he likes now, and he tries to concentrate.

"Mommy, I want to touch him," one child says.

"Look at the cake," says another, who's sitting on the railing to Tandolfo's right, with a new pair of shiny binoculars trained on the car. "Do we get some cake?"

"There's cake," says the man in the DAD cap. "But not that cake. Get down, Ethan."

"I want that cake."

"Get down. This is Teddy's birthday."

"Mommy, I want to touch him."

"I need a table, folks. I told somebody that over the telephone."

"He did say he needed a table. I'm sorry," says a woman who is probably the birthday boy's mother. She's quite pretty, leaning in the doorframe with a sweater tied to her waist.

"A table," says another woman. Tandolfo sees the birthmark on her mouth, which looks like a stain. He thinks of this woman as a child in school, with this difference from other children, and his heart goes out to her.

"I need a table," he says to her, his voice as gentle as he can make it.

"What's he going to do, perform an operation?" says DAD.

It amazes Tandolfo how easily people fall into talking about him as though he were an inanimate object, or something on a television screen. "The Great Tandolfo can do nothing until he gets a table," he says, with as much mysteriousness and drama as he can muster under the circumstances.

"I want that cake out there," says Ethan, still perched atop the porch railing. The other children start talking about cake and ice cream, and the big cake Ethan has spotted; there's a lot of confusion, and restlessness. One of the smaller children, a girl in a blue dress, comes forward and stands gazing at Tandolfo. "What's your name?" she says, swaying slightly, her hands behind her back.

"Go sit down," he says to her. "We have to sit down or Tandolfo can't do his magic."

In the doorway, two of the men are struggling with a folding card table. It's one of those rickety ones with the skinny legs, and it won't do.

"That's kind of rickety, isn't it?" says the woman with the birthmark.

"I said Tandolfo needs a sturdy table, boys and girls."

There's more confusion. The little girl has come forward and taken hold of his pant leg. She's just standing there holding it, looking at him. "We have to go sit down," he says, bending to her, speaking sweetly, clownlike. "We have to do what Tandolfo wants."

Her small mouth opens wide, as if she's trying to yawn, and with pale blue eyes quite calm and staring she emits a screech, an ear-piercing, nonhuman shriek that brings everything to a stop. Tandolfo/Rodney steps back, with his amazement and his inebriate heart, and now everyone's gathering around the girl, who continues to scream, less piercing now, her hands fisted at her sides, those blue eyes closed tight.

"What happened?" the man in the DAD cap wants to know. "Where the hell's the magic tricks?"

"I told you all I needed a *table*."

"Whud you say to her to make her cry?" He indicates the little girl, who is not merely crying but is giving forth a series of broken, grief-stricken howls.

"I want magic tricks," the birthday boy says, loud. "Where's the magic tricks?"

"Perhaps if we moved the whole thing inside," the woman with the birthmark says, fingering her left ear and making a face.

The card table has somehow made its way to Tandolfo, through the confusion and grief. The man in the DAD cap sets it down and opens it.

"There," he says, as if his point is made.

In the next moment, Tandolfo realizes that someone's removed the little girl. Everything's relatively quiet again, though her cries are coming through the walls of one of the rooms inside the house. There are perhaps fifteen children, mostly seated before him; five or six men and women behind them, or kneeling with them. "Okay, now," DAD says. "Tandolfo the Great."

"Hello, little boys and girls," Tandolfo/Rodney says. "I'm happy to be here. Are you glad to see me?" A general uproar goes up. "Well, good," he says. "Because just look what I have in my magic bag." And with a flourish, he brings out the hat from which he will release Witch. The bird is encased inside a fold of shiny cloth, pulsing there. He can feel it. He rambles on, talking fast, or trying to, and when the time comes to reveal the bird, he almost flubs it. But Witch flaps his wings and makes enough of a commotion to distract even the adults, who applaud now, and get the children to applaud. "Isn't that wonderful," Tandolfo hears. "Where did that bird come from?"

"He had it hidden away," says the birthday boy.

"Now," Tandolfo says, "for my next spell, I need a little friend from the audience." He looks right at the birthday boy—round face; short nose; freckles. Bright red hair. Little green eyes. The whole countenance speaks of glutted appetites and sloth. This kid could be on Roman coins, an emperor. He's not used to being compelled to do anything, but he seems eager for a chance to get into the act. "How about you?" Tandolfo says to him.

The others, led by their parents, cheer.

The birthday boy gets to his feet and makes his way over the bodies of the other children to stand with Tandolfo. In order for the trick to work, Tandolfo must get everyone watching the birthday boy, and there's a funny hat he keeps in the bag for this purpose. "Now," he says to the boy, "since you're part of the show, you have to wear a costume." He produces the hat as if from behind the boy's ear. Another cheer goes up. He puts the hat on his head and adjusts it, crouching down. The green eyes stare impassively at him; there's no hint of awe or fascination in them. "There we are," he says. "What a handsome fellow."

But the birthday boy takes the hat off.

"No, no. We have to wear the hat to be onstage."

"Ain't a stage," the boy says.

"Well, but hey," Tandolfo says for the benefit of the adults. "Didn't you know that all the world's a stage?" He tries to put the hat on again, but the boy moves from under his reach and slaps his hand away. "We have to wear the hat," Tandolfo says, trying to control his anger. "We can't do the magic without our magic hats." He tries once more, and the boy waits until the hat is on, then simply removes it and holds it behind him, shying away when Tandolfo tries to retrieve it. The noise of the others now sounds like the crowd at a prizefight; there's a contest going on, and they're enjoying it. "Give Tandolfo the hat now. We want magic, don't we?"

"Do the magic," the boy demands.

"I'll do the magic if you give me the hat."

"I won't."

Nothing. No support from the adults. Perhaps if he weren't a little tipsy, perhaps if he didn't feel ridiculous and sick at heart and forlorn, with his wedding cake and his odd mistaken romance, his loneliness, which he has always borne gracefully and in humor, and his general dismay; perhaps if he were to find it in himself to deny the sudden, overwhelming sense of the unearned affection given this little slovenly version of stupid complacent spoiled satiation standing before him—he might've simply gone on to the next trick.

Instead, he leans down and in the noise of the moment, says to the boy, "Give me the hat, you little prick."

The green eyes widen slightly.

It grows quiet. Even the small children can tell that something's happened to change everything.

"Tandolfo has another trick," Rodney says, "where he makes the birthday boy pop like a balloon. Especially if he's a fat birthday boy."

A stirring among the adults.

"Especially if he's an ugly little slab of flesh like this one here."

"Now just a minute," says DAD.

"Pop," Rodney says to the birthday boy, who drops the hat and then, seeming to remember that defiance is expected, makes a face. Sticks out his tongue. Rodney/Tandolfo is quick with his hands by training, and he grabs the tongue.

"Awk," the boy says. "Aw-aw-aw."

"Abracadabra." Rodney lets go, and the boy falls backward into the lap of one of the older children. "Whoops, time to sit down," says Rodney.

Very quickly, he's being forcibly removed. They're rougher than gangsters. They lift him, punch him, tear at his costume —even the women. Someone hits him with a spoon. The whole scene boils out onto the lawn, where someone has released the case that Chi-Chi was in. Chi-Chi moves about wide-eyed, hopping between running children, evading them, as Tandolfo the Great cannot evade the adults. He's being pummeled, because he keeps trying to return for his rabbit. And the adults won't let him off the curb.

"Okay," he says finally, collecting himself. He wants to let them know he's not like this all the time; wants to say it's circumstances, grief, personal pain hidden inside seeming brightness and cleverness; he's a man in love, humiliated, wrong about everything. He wants to tell them, but he can't speak for a moment, can't even quite catch his breath. He stands in the middle of the street, his funny clothes torn, his face bleeding, all his magic strewn everywhere. "I would at least like to collect my rabbit," he says, and is appalled at the absurd sound of it— its huge difference from what he intended to say. He straightens, pushes the hair out of his eyes, adjusts the clown nose, and looks at them. "I would say that even though I wasn't as patient as I could've been, the adults have not comported themselves well here," he says.

"Drunk," one of the women says.

Almost everyone's chasing Chi-Chi now. One of the older boys approaches him, carrying Witch's case. Witch looks out the air hole, impervious, quiet as an idea. And now one of the men, someone Tandolfo hasn't noticed before, an older man clearly wearing a hairpiece, brings Chi-Chi to him. "Bless you," Rodney says, staring into the man's sleepy, deploring gaze.

"I don't think we'll pay you," the man says. The others are all filing back into the house, herding the children before them.

Rodney speaks to the man. "The rabbit appears out of fire."

The man nods. "Go home and sleep it off, kid."

"Right, thank you."

He puts Chi-Chi in his compartment, stuffs everything in its place in the trunk. Then he gets in and drives away. Around the corner he stops, wipes off what he can of the makeup; it's as if he's trying to remove the grime of bad opinion and disapproval. Nothing feels any different. He drives to the little suburban street where she lives with her parents, and by the time he gets there it's almost dark. The houses are set back in the trees; he sees lighted windows, hears music, the sound of children playing in the yards. He parks the car and gets out. A breezy April dusk.

"I am Tandolfo the soft-hearted," he says. "Hearken to me." Then he sobs. He can't believe it. "Jeez," he says. "Goddam."

He opens the back door of the car, leans in to get the cake. He'd forgotten how heavy it is. Staggering with it, making his way along the sidewalk, intending to leave it on her doorstep, he has an inspiration. Hesitating only for the moment it takes to make sure there are no cars coming, he goes out and sets it down in the middle of the street.

Part of the top sags slightly, from having bumped his shoulder as he pulled it off the backseat of the car. The bride and groom are almost supine, one on top of the other. He straightens them, steps back, and looks at it. In the dusky light, it looks blue. It sags just right, with just the right angle, expressing disappointment and sorrow.

Yes, he thinks. This is the place for it. The aptness of it, sitting out like this, where anyone might come by and splatter it all over creation, actually makes him feel some faint sense of release, as if he were at the end of a story. Everything will be all right if he can think of it that way. He's wiping his eyes, thinking of moving to another town. There are money troubles and troubles at work, and failures beginning to catch up to him, and he's still aching in love. He thinks how he has suffered the pangs of failure and misadventure, but in this painful instance there's symmetry, and he will make the one eloquent gesture—leaving a wedding cake in the middle of the road, like a sugar-icinged pylon. Yes.

He walks back to the car, gets in, pulls it around, and backs into the driveway of the house across the street. Leaving the engine idling, he rolls the window down and rests his arm on the sill, gazing at the incongruous shape of it there in the falling dark. He feels almost glad, almost—in some strange inexpressible way—vindicated, and he imagines what she might do if she saw him here. In a moment he's fantasizing that she comes running from her house, calling his name, looking at the cake and admiring it. This fantasy gives way to something else: images of destruction, flying sugar and candy debris. He's quite surprised to find that he wants her to stay where she is, doing whatever she's doing. He realizes with a feeling akin to elation that what he really wants—and for the moment all he really wants—is what he now has: a perfect vantage point from which to watch oncoming cars.

Turning the engine off, he waits, concentrating on the one thing, full of anticipation—dried blood and grime on his face, his hair all on end, his eyes glazed with rage and humiliation—a man imbued with interest, and happily awaiting the results of his labor.

Bells

JOSEPHINE HUMPHREYS

For a time I didn't want to be myself but could think of no way out. The things I tried, eyeglasses and therapy, were having no deep effect. Still, I didn't give them up but thought of them as spells laid to court the future. I wanted to become a person not beset by desire or fear or hope.

Children long for that change, to be strong at last. That's why my second-graders liked me; we had in common a secret need, so I never thought of them as tiresome and never spoke to them as if to inferior beings. A group of them, mostly girls, stayed with me at recess, not hanging on my skirt or holding my hand but close enough to keep me in sight. It was the part of the school day I liked best, when we were outside. I don't think emotions can run rampant in the open daylight air the way they can inside

a house (or worse, in bed at night). When I was in the schoolyard
I felt okay or better, with the breeze through the live oaks, the
dirt yard white and hard as rock, and the second-graders all around
me.

I tried to tell Jeffcoat I wasn't so alone as he thought, I wasn't
cutting myself off from the rest of the world as he said. The
company of children is in many ways a truer, more honest company than can be found elsewhere, I said. But he raised his
eyebrows. Maybe he didn't agree or he didn't believe me or he
thought my students were only substitutes for children I didn't
have of my own.

It was very hard to explain myself.

When I'd first seen his sign, "Pastoral Counseling," I thought
of something quiet and green. It suited me that he was not a
psychiatrist. I didn't want to be treated by science. I wanted to
find out if one human being could simply drop in on another
and ask for help and get it even when the trouble could not be
put into so many words.

He was not bad at counseling but he was not immediately
good. While I talked I kept thinking he ought to be more alert
for nuances. He missed things. Worse, he couldn't tell when I
was lying and when I was not, and until he learned to do that I
didn't think we could make progress. But there was a leafy su-
garberry tree outside his window, and the office was quiet. Jeffcoat, thin and bearded and blue-eyed, had a promising air about
him, even though at first he wasn't on the right track. Like my
parents, he said if I would get out more and see people, adults,
I would feel better. To him I was a twenty-four-year-old divorced
teacher who needed to face facts and proceed with life. My ex-
husband's imminent remarriage in June was the fact I had to face
and "move past," Jeffcoat said.

The theory was not wrong but it was incomplete. It was missing the bout of promiscuity that had come on me like a flu and that I could not fight off or understand. I ought to have mentioned it to him but I could not. Jeffcoat was innocent and Presbyterian, past fifty at least, and maybe such things were beyond his imagination. To tell him outright could have harmed him.

"What about those options we discussed last week?" he said. He was a handsome man and shy the way preachers sometimes are. He didn't look directly at me. "You were going to take some steps toward, as we said, getting rid of baggage." The terms he used showed he thought of life as something similar to a hike and you were supposed to move steadily forward on it but I was stalled.

That divorce had been my fault, I admitted. I had messed up the marriage with fear and weakness. All it ever was was me whining and not letting Joe be. Why did he have to work late, why didn't he give me more presents—these things I had said partly joking, acting this sort of wifely role that was half real and half game. I was a brat with Joe and didn't love him desperately until he was gone. We were married for less than a year. That kind of flash-in-the-pan marriage, people can see, was a mistake from the onset, and no one will really blame you for it; but it is not the kind of thing that bolsters your self-confidence.

Then for a time I believed he would come back. Even after we were legally divorced and you would think I'd have given up, I still had blind faith that he would return. I had *improved*, so why should he not give me a second try? I didn't hound him; far from it, I didn't even contact him, hoping, I guess, that news of my reformation would reach him through the town network, and he'd show up at my place one night. Not until I heard about him and Rebecca did I wake up. And all the hope that had been focused on Joe suddenly had nowhere to go and so went everywhere. That's how I put it to Jeffcoat, without being more explicit.

At Jeffcoat's suggestion I'd agreed to throw away all souvenirs, the photos and letters, the coat Joe left in the closet, and the top layer of my wedding cake which had been quietly freezing in the refrigerator, its pair of white sugar bells canted, supposedly in the middle of a bong.

"I did it," I said. "Put everything in the street. The garbagemen hauled it away."

"You've been wanting to do that for some time, but you thought it would be difficult."

"It was easy."

He took notes during the sessions. I couldn't help thinking that in the end there would be a written story, a work of literature. The thought of the growing story kept me talking. When his pen lifted to wait for more details, I gave them.

"It was beautiful," I said, my eye on the motion of his hand, my only hint—since he rested the notepad at an angle between the desktop and his thigh—of what he might be writing.

"You felt good about it."

"No, I mean it was beautiful, the pile of stuff—Joe's old coat still in the dry-cleaning plastic, and the pictures set around it and the cake on top. It looked like art. I watched through the window to see what people thought when they came by. It caught their eye but no one bothered it because it looked like it had been done on purpose. Even the garbagemen hesitated. I had to go out and tell them to take it. People respect something that looks arranged and intentional. They think it means something."

"And—did it?"

"To me?"

"Yes."

I weighed my words, closing my eyes, trying to see the cake there. "I don't know. It was a way to make sense of things that don't make sense. The idea behind it was to throw away the old and prepare for the new." He wrote, but he was still in the dark.

I didn't mind. I liked talking, choosing words for things that were partly true and waiting to see if they sounded wholly true. And I liked talking to someone who had no personal stake in me, who was like an anonymous listener, someone I wouldn't have to go back to if I didn't want to. Jeffcoat was a proper audience. My parents were not; they had just moved into a new place and were energetic and optimistic, and I didn't want to disturb that. If they had found out what was happening to me they would have been dismayed. It had been a year since my divorce, and they thought I was okay. I tried to act normal with them, but one afternoon in the courtyard of their new townhouse Dad was showing me his tomato plants and I felt about to cry for no reason except the way things looked: the pale green plants in their wooden tubs, the patio furniture bright in the May sun, my dad in his white shirt and khaki pants and canvas shoes. I was frightened because I hadn't had this happen to me in the out-of-doors before.

"Are you okay, Millie?" he said. Palmettos rattled in the courtyard, their fronds dry and stiff. "Are you working too hard?" he said.

I knew I wouldn't answer truthfully but maybe I could say something like "I've been feeling kind of low," and then he might talk me into staying for supper and I wouldn't have to go back to my apartment until late. But my mother came out with iced tea. She looked crisp and clean in her white pleated skirt. It made me feel stronger, to see how strong she was.

"I'm doing all right," I said to Dad. "School will be out soon, and I'll be able to take it easy."

However, I dreaded the summer vacation, when I would be stuck in my apartment complex with the pool and the people who came and went. In summers I was bereaved, missing the schoolchildren. And I worried about who was caring for them in the summer months. They would be sent to mountain camp, swimming lessons, vacation Bible school, and then return to school slightly hardened, slightly tougher. They would have learned to hide themselves better.

"What a nice surprise," Mother said, pouring me tea with chunks of lemon in the bottom of the tumbler. "We don't see enough of you, darling." Her legs were sleek with nylon, her hair shiny and pulled back with combs. She leaned to me over the patio table, her face coming into the shadow of the blue umbrella. "How's your love life?" she said.

"Fine."

"You're playing the field?" Dad said.

It was such an old-fashioned expression I couldn't help laughing. I thought about baseball teams. Mother stood up, smoothing her skirt. "Promise me you're really going out and seeing people," she said.

"I promise."

"I like your glasses," she said.

"They don't do anything. They're a disguise."

"How about supper?" Dad said. "Want to stay and eat? We have shrimp." He stood behind Mother and put his hands on her shoulders. They had been married for thirty years. They had never had trouble in their lives, nothing had gone wrong for them.

"Can't. I have tests to grade." I got up and moved out from under the umbrella, wishing I could look clean and smooth.

"Millie, before you go—"

"Yes?"

"I heard Joe's marrying Rebecca Whitman."

"Yes?"

"I was just a little worried that it might upset you."

"No," I said.

"The past is over and done with," my father said.

"Right, Dad." I kissed his cheek.

"Good," Mother said.

When I left I drove around for a while in my air-conditioned car, not wanting to go home but feeling better than usual, I guess because my parents were healthy and happy and trusted me to be the same.

In the apartment I undressed and turned the air conditioner to high. I put on a bathing suit and sat on the bed to grade spelling tests. After six of them I got up and went out to the pool. There was a man on the diving board I recognized. He didn't live here but sometimes came to swim, which is how I'd met him. I didn't want to be with him again, I didn't want him to see me, but I watched from a distance as he walked out onto the diving board and sprang and dove, shooting to the bottom and then curving up, breaking out and shaking the water from his head. I remembered also that this man had been kind and funny, and very strong; he had been surprised when I wouldn't see him again.

What I wanted from him or from any man was not something he could donate to me like love, but something I might steal—the courage of the dive, the plunge into solitude, the singularity. I'm sorry I can't say more exactly what it was. Somewhere tribes believe an animal's heart strengthens the person who consumes it, and I doubt the tribes can explain why. I had not been able to tell Jeffcoat about the men because it would have sounded like despair, when it was the opposite. I hoped for something, I hoped for everything, from the men I saw. Despair would have been much easier than what I had, hope wildly out of control.

It was five o'clock. I went back inside, where the spelling tests were still on the bed. In the kitchen, I opened the freezer to get ice and saw the wedding bells still freezing and then through the window the man still diving. He was a medical student, unmarried, a good man; which was why I hadn't wanted to see him a second time. And why I walked back out to the pool and invited him in. After he left I called my mother, but there was no answer.

I wanted to tell her and tell Jeffcoat something I could not get at except by lying. It is easy enough to say facts: the twenty-four-year-old teacher, the failed marriage, the husband's remarriage, all of which were true but seemed so distant from me as to be false. How do you say that a fact can be something else, even its opposite—loneliness love and despair hope?

Every week, more and more of what I told Jeffcoat was technically untrue. School let out, June came. Coincidentally, on the day of Joe's wedding I had a session with Jeffcoat, during which every word out of my mouth was false. It quite exhausted me, that much relentless fiction, but it exhilarated me as well. Nothing was overdone, nothing was suspiciously perfect, but all approximated reality so closely that now and then he glanced up from writing with a look of satisfaction, even of gratitude. I said I was pretty happy, I no longer thought of Joe except in general and friendly terms, I had learned to separate emotionally from the children at school, I had met a man I liked who was a swimmer and who seemed to like me and I was looking forward to seeing him again. I painted a picture of life making sense.

At the end of the hour, Jeffcoat stopped me. I had been talking fast and he'd had to write nonstop. He sank into private thinking and let me go.

So I was surprised the next week when he said he didn't think I needed to see him anymore. "I believe you're out of the danger zone, and moving in the right direction," he said.

I was slouched in his leather club chair. In our three months together we had become casual in our posture; now he had rocked his desk chair back on two legs and was staring out the window. We had also grown accustomed to a strange reluctance, on both sides, to quit at the end of the hour. Sometimes a long silence would come, and neither of us felt the need to fill it. One came now. We didn't speak or move for five minutes.

Then I said, "But I haven't told you everything."

He laughed. "What did you leave out?"

"Well—"

"You see," he said, "it doesn't matter. It would be impossible to tell everything." He looked sure of what he said. I sat there for a minute at a loss.

"And also I haven't told the truth."

"You're a strong young woman," he said.

"What makes you think that?"

"Because you tell a good strong lie." His chair came forward and he turned his pale eyes on me. The thing was, he was a really good man. I liked him intensely, and we had come to mean something to each other, but not like what you usually think of: not lovers, not father-daughter or doctor-patient, but something else, which had to end. "That cake is still in your freezer, isn't it?" he said.

"No, I threw it away. I told you that. Months ago."

He smiled.

I have always made it a habit to tell my students they are smart and good because I know that words sink in. It is a kind of trick that maybe a teacher should not use, and I would never have thought it could be used on me and work. But hearing him say I was out of the danger zone, a sure falsehood, made me feel good.

He said to feel free to drop by if I ever needed to and I said I would. I left his office and took a long time walking out to the street, stopping for a minute under the pastoral counseling sign, half believing everything I had told. Jeffcoat was rare. I had chosen him almost at random, accidentally, and he had turned out to be just right: an amazing coincidence.

Of course we knew that I'd never be out of the danger zone, and neither would he or anyone who thought much. But I had toughened up some. What we had become was people who tell stories to each other. That was the way it worked.

To Guess the Riddle,
to Stumble on a Secret Name

GEORGE GARRETT

A little past noon on a fine spring day. A man, the professor, is driving to school, tooling along the freeway.

"In his Porsche," she says.

I don't see where that's relevant. It's a detail we can do without.

"It's the most relevant thing about him," she says, "and it was half mine before the divorce."

Who's telling this story? I say.

"It's his story, but you go ahead and tell it anyway."

Okay, so the professor is driving along at a pretty good clip when all of a sudden this car passes him. A beat-up, rattly, old, gas-guzzling heap, pumping out a cloud of pollutants.

With shoes and tin cans tied on the back and all the usual

"Just Married" graffiti painted all over it. And then the car cuts him off. Swerves back into his lane and he damn near has to ride right up the back of it. So he leans on his horn. And then at the back window lo and behold there is the blushing bride herself, wearing her bridal gown, a very pretty girl with wild bright eyes and a great big smile. And she is giving him the finger and calling him every name in the book.

She says: "How can he hear her?"

He's a lip reader. Everybody's reading everybody else's lips these days.

She goes: "Read mine."

Then: "Is that all there is to it? I mean, it's a pretty simple story for Mark. Brief and simple things just don't happen to him."

What happens next is the guy in the heap, the groom I guess, cranks up and just leaves him in the dust and smoke. Must have been doing a hundred easy. Mark tries to tailgate him for a while. Notices that the muffler is hanging loose and about to fall off any minute. Then the Westside exit comes up and he has to slow down to turn off. And here, right behind him, comes a whole convoy of cars, all of them blowing their horns like crazy and chasing after the bride and groom.

He's already pulling into the college parking lot before he wonders what in the world the bride was doing in the backseat.

She says: "Everybody's got to be somewhere. Even a bride."

So, anyway, he teaches his classes and then has a couple of appointments at his office.

And she says—"Cute little flat-tummied coeds who all call him Mark and tell him how much they love learning about all these different things like minimalism and postmodern meta-fiction and stuff like that."

Don't be bitter.

She says: "Why not?"

So I shrug and go on: He picks up his mail and heads for home.

When he gets back to the freeway, on pure impulse, he decides to go in the other way to follow the direction the wedding party had been going. He doesn't know why, he just wants to. And that's how he happens to find it.

"Find what?" She asks.

A wedding cake. Notice that I did *not* say *the* wedding cake. Because there is nothing whatsoever to connect this particular wedding cake with that particular bride who gave him the finger some hours ago, just the resonance and sychronicity of things. But there it is, anyway, in the big middle of the grass median. Just sitting there—a perfect three-tiered wedding cake, undamaged, more like it was just *put there* than dropped or lost.

She says: "Purposefully abandoned, you might say."

Mark parks in the breakdown lane. And when there is a little space in the traffic he sprints across to the median. Chases away a couple of hungry crows. Then kneels down to get a good look at it. This cake has something weird about it. At first he can only *feel* the weirdness, but then he finally sees what it is. On top there is the usual candy bride, but there are also *two* little candy grooms. Two little candy grooms just standing there side by side.

"Maybe she was marrying Siamese twins," she says. Then: "I don't believe a word of it."

Mark didn't think anybody would. So he ran back to the car and got his Polaroid and took pictures. Here. Proof. See for yourself.

"I don't have to," she says, shaking her lovely head and sounding almost happy, smiling now as if she had suddenly guessed a riddle or stumbled on the secret name—Rumpelstiltskin!

She says: "It's the kind of thing that always happens to him.

Mark's nasty little world is full of misery and mischief, and he likes to share it with other people."

Give the guy a break.

"I did already," she says, "one time too many."

Then with an abrupt vehemence, something close to fury she says, "Don't you see? He wants to make trouble for us. The whole thing is a message to me. And the beauty of it is that he got you to deliver the message for him.

"And what's the message?" She continues, "Simple enough. That, divorce or no divorce, wedding cake or not, he'll never let me go."

You really hate him, don't you? I say, hoping that it's true, hoping I won't have to hear the answer that, in fact, I do.

"No," she is saying. "I don't hate him. I never did and I guess I never will."

Dogs

MARY LEE SETTLE

Mrs. Webster says that she remembers when only large Southern families who belonged there lived on Chatham, Dunmore, and North streets. In 1900, it was a new subdivision, carved out of the last farm left within the city limits of Norfolk, Virginia. The streets were all named for members of the House of Lords. The front lawns were all alike, and everyone kept servants who were underpaid.

In old photographs it still looks like raw and naked farmland with spindly trees defining the new roads. Now the trees almost meet over the streets. The huge solid houses have aged into brick and stone monuments to a past when everyone was "well off" and life was supposed to be more stable. I don't believe it was, because a residue of the times remains and can be read like books about Southern stereotypes, when relatives lived together and got on each other's nerves, old women developed strange habits, men committed suicide when they lost their money or their minds, and plain people were no kin. The whole district is now on the Historic Register, and nobody can put up a fence or a garage without the approval of a committee appointed by the city council. This makes Mrs. Webster absolutely furious.

Some of the facades have Sir Walter Scott towers, some are Banker's Edwardian. There are Swiss-chalet porches, mansard roofs, and ornamental chimneys, but all the details are different icing on the same basic cake.

Inside, under twelve-foot ceilings, behind fourteen-inch-thick walls, you can read the changes in the neighborhood by the colors. In the houses that the young parents have bought, there are dark green or red or lemon-yellow rooms with bright white woodwork and ceilings. The walls are splashed with modern paintings. The parents play catch with their children in the front yards. In the early evening the games spill out into the street, and there is the sound of Mrs. Webster's window being slammed shut, mingled with the birdcalls of children in the twilight. Mrs. Webster is eighty-four and she rules a kingdom that no longer exists, except in echoes and hints.

Her house, like the houses of the few old people who are left, still has cream ceilings and woodwork that have turned the color of dust. The living room and the dining room are the same dull cream and green gone sad, history in a color scheme. Cream and green were the colors of harmony in the early twenties when, as soon as their parents died, the then-young reacted to the dark damask walls of the older generation and brought Ricketts and Shannon into fashion thirty years after they had revolutionized the dark interiors of London and painted Oscar Wilde's house in Tite Street. Now, in England, cream and green are Ministry of Works, Scheme E, used for prison walls. On Chatham, Dunmore, and North streets, they are the faded symbol of polite revolt a long time ago. The wall sconces have bulbs shaped like candles and opaque parchment shades that clamp onto them like angry jaws.

Outside the houses that have not changed hands, the shrubs are thick with flat, oily leaves, and the holly is mean and prickly to keep children away. The heavy planting has long since become a thieves' shelter, but the old don't recognize this. Mrs. Webster talks about a time when there were no robberies. She says nobody would have dared.

Mrs. Webster, whose father was an Episcopal clergyman and whose mother was a Carver, still lives in the house where she was born on Dunmore Street. She says she was the first child born there, with her voice a little hushed, as if she were as historic as Virginia Dare.

She remembers every change, every marriage, every scandal. There were never very many on Dunmore Street, but she makes of them what she can. She once led The German, which was the ball where every girl (she says "gel") in the Three Streets came out at the Yacht Club. Then she adds, "Well, almost every gel." There is a yellowed picture of her when she was seventeen in a white beaded dress. She is holding flowers and crinkling her eyes and smiling. The frame is silver and it sits on a Duncan Phyfe table that belongs in the family. It is a charming picture. She still smiles like that, crinkling her eyes. She says she was told once by a beau that her smile was devastating. Then she adds, "It's a crying shame the boys don't pay compliments anymore. The gels don't know what they miss."

You can see her on sunny days in spring, her behind tilted up in the air, worrying her cerise azaleas, which are like small trees. She wears a man's shirt left over from Mr. Webster, and gardening gloves, and one of those wrap-around denim skirts she sends away for to the same mail-order house she has always used. On late afternoons in summer, when a breeze has finally risen from the surface of the ornamental water that nearly surrounds the oasis of the Three Streets, she wears a sweet, frilly blouse and a flowered skirt, and makes her eyes crinkle when you meet her on her daily walk.

Everyone in the neighborhood keeps dogs, and it is by the breeds that they choose that you know them and their politics. The cream-and-green conservatives expel onto front porches fat, aging spaniels and little barking terriers in defiance of the leash law that did not exist when they were young. Mrs. Webster's dog is an insane mongrel bitch she says is part terrier, called Bounce.

"Our dogs," she says, as if there have always been a pack of hounds, instead of one inevitable dog that has looked like its predecessor for years, "are always called Bounce."

The lawns of the young are spaced with softly colored flowering shrubs and spring bulbs. Their houses all have burglar alarms.

In the liberal houses there are large purebred poodles, golden retrievers, Dalmatians, and English setters. In two of the houses there are more ominous German shepherds and Dobermans that their owners refuse to put on leashes, as if they needed their animal power to control the streets.

One man, Mr. Tripp, has both a German shepherd and a Doberman. He patrols with them in the early afternoon as if he expected an invasion of Dunmore Street. He hollers, "Hyuh, Beau," and "Hyuh, Stu," in the voice of the upwardly mobile South. He is seventy-three and he once worked for the CIA. He is still mysterious about this.

Mrs. Webster pretends he doesn't exist. So does Bounce, the only dog that doesn't bark to get into the house when it hears Mr. Tripp coming.

There is one house on Dunmore Street where there are no dogs. Mrs. MacArthur lives there. Mrs. Webster says that she and her husband, "a jumped-up rear admiral, the war, you know," bought the house in 1950. She says Mrs. MacArthur was forty then if she was a day, but she still tried to look like June Allyson. "Her husband," she says, "was simply years older," and then adds, "I don't know what they expected.

"They were from New Jersey," she almost whispers, and then, "She wore slacks with high-heeled shoes."

Admiral MacArthur retired a few years later. They had a daughter who grew up on Dunmore Street. "But of course," Mrs. Webster says, "they never really took part." That remark, translated, means that their daughter did not come out at The German, and that the MacArthurs, like Mr. Tripp, were treated as if they did not exist. "After all," Mrs. Webster says, "there were always so many Navy people.

"When the daughter married for the first time, but always into the Navy, I'll say that for her"—Mrs. Webster tells the story, doing her devastating crinkle—"they asked everybody in the neighborhood to the wedding. It was quite embarrassing. We discussed it. We honestly didn't know what to do about it. I suppose they do that kind of thing in New Jersey. They had the reception at *home.* Can you imagine? I mean, not even the Navy mess or whatever they call it.

"The morning of the wedding I was out teaching Bounce to stay out of the street. She was only two then and just the dearest little thing. The van from the bakery stopped in front of the MacArthurs' house and Bounce saw the delivery man. He was carrying a huge wedding cake in a box. Bounce ran across the road and bit him in the leg. I felt terrible about that part, the delivery man had to have those shots, but of course the insurance paid. But then, Bounce was so funny I couldn't help laughing. When the box flew open and the wedding cake dropped right into the middle of the road, she ate the groom before I could grab her. After that I really thought I ought to go to the wedding and take a little present by the house, but of course I didn't stay. Mrs. MacArthur was very cool to me even after I apologized profusely."

Now Mrs. MacArthur's daughter lives with her third husband in California. (Maybe if Bounce hadn't eaten the groom off of that cake, her luck in men might have been better.) When the admiral was still alive the daughter sent her son by her first husband back to live on Dunmore Street. The admiral died eight years ago. Mrs. Webster thought she ought to go to the funeral at All Saints, although she did point out the MacArthurs were never very active there. She was the only person who wore white gloves and carried her own 1928 Prayer Book. All through the new service, she flipped the pages, annoyed. Afterwards she said she just didn't know. "Until the day he died, he never let her write a check or drive a car. He waited on her hand and foot. She didn't even wear black."

Now only Mrs. MacArthur and her grandson live in the house on Dunmore Street, still marooned there among strangers. He is twenty-three and unemployed. He is building a boat in the driveway which he plans to sail across the Atlantic the other way. At night the arc welder he uses lights the trees with a weird white glare.

They imitate the Southerners they think surround them, as victims imitate their oppressors for camouflage. Their shrubs are oily and prickly, their walls are cream and green, and at night their shades are drawn tight, not against the new paranoid fear of rapists, but the old one of neighbors and, most of all, their dogs.

Outside of the arc welder, Mrs. MacArthur's major concession to modern life is the telephone. "She has one in nearly every room," Mrs. Webster says. At the briefest bark from any dog in the neighborhood, the telephone inside the dog owner's house rings. When it is answered there is one of those silences, fraught not with heavy breathing, but with electric fury.

When it all began, neighbors thought burglars were checking to see if they were at home, so every month or so a new dog was added to the neighborhood pack until Mrs. MacArthur succeeded in surrounding herself with a canine siege. The dogs seem to know something. They pull at their leashes until they get to her shrubs. Their owners have let them turn the leaves brown.

All of the neighbors now know what Mrs. MacArthur is doing, and since they are easygoing people they leave her alone, except for the brown bushes. But her ears have become so acute that even a bark *inside* a neighbor's house brings the inevitable telephone call, as regular as clockwork, as well timed as a television commercial. Once, in fact, a commercial for dog food triggered five calls in rapid succession from Mrs. MacArthur to neighbors watching a *M.A.S.H.* rerun.

Mrs. MacArthur's hair is a bird's nest. She wears tennis shoes without stockings and a wraparound denim skirt like Mrs. Webster's winter and summer, day and night. She speaks to nobody. If she were poor and in a large city, she would be accosting people in the street, shouting obscenities. On Dunmore Street the phones ring. Around her the neighbors are amused, and as cruel as only the indifferent can be. They are tolerant, which means nobody knows what to do about her or cares.

"Children bark now as they walk past her house on their way home from school," Mrs. Webster says. Mrs. MacArthur's calls follow them all over the neighborhood. Five years ago she bought a pale yellow cat and had it neutered. It has grown huge. It sits on her doorstep in the sun and attracts dog barks. Methodically she lets it out and then goes and sits by the telephone, waiting. In the daytime you can see her through the organdy curtains.

Possum

CHARLES BAXTER

The girl, Helena, was almost twice as old as her brother, Hector, and she considered herself twice as smart, although it was hard for her to judge, because he was young and therefore just naturally stupid. Plus, he was a boy, which made him brain-damaged from birth. She had nine years to his five, and, riding in the backseat in the middle of July, she had already tricked him out of his two quarters and his half of an M&M's package. She had told him that for fifty cents and some candy she would give him a snipe —a soft furry animal that would sleep with him at night—once they got home, in Illinois. They were still crossing Ohio. She said Ohio should be outlawed, it was so flat and boring.

Up front, their father was driving and listening to his Walkman. Their mother was irritably sleeping.

Helena was an inventive and forceful bully, skilled at creating games only she could win. "Let's play 'Wzzat,' " she said, taking out the last M&M, a green one.

"What's 'Wzzat'?"

"Okay okay, I'll explain," she said, raising her eyes to the ceiling, as if everyone in the world except Hector knew how to play. "You close your eyes. You know how to do that, don't you?"

"Yes."

"Okay. You close your eyes. Then I look out the window, and I see real things, but I can make up things, too. And so I say, 'There's a horse.' And you can either challenge me, and say 'I challenge you,' and if there's a horse there, you lose. You get it?"

Hector nodded, even though Helena could see that he didn't get it at all.

"But maybe I make up things, right? And you can challenge me, and if it's not there, I lose, and then you get to be It. I mean, it's so simple even you can get it."

"I *don't* get it," he whined.

"Okay okay," she said. "I'll close my eyes." She half-closed them, so she could detect a bit of something. "Now you look around, and if you notice anything, you can say what you see, or you can make it all up."

There was a long silence. At last Hector said, "I think I see a dog."

Helena could tell that there *was* a dog, an ugly black dog half a mile out in a farmer's field. "That's good," she said. "You get it. But the deal is, I wouldn't *challenge* you about that."

"I'm not finished," Hector said. "It's a dog from Mars."

"No, it isn't." Her eyes flew open like tightly sprung window shades. "It's just a dog."

"How do *you* know?" Hector asked. "I think it's from Mars. It looked a lot like a Martian dog."

"What do dogs from Mars look like?"

"Like that one." Hector smiled. "They have outer-space ears."

Helena sighed and raised her eyes to the ceiling again. She couldn't imagine being married to a human being with a penis, if her brother was any example of what she'd have to put up with. "Never mind," she said. "Close your eyes. If you don't believe me, just say, 'I challenge.' You got it?"

"I think so."

"All right. There's a fence."

"I challenge."

"Too bad. There's a fence there. See that stupid-looking fence?"

"I guess so."

"Close your eyes again." She waited until Hector did so. She was feeling full of power and evil. "There's a llama."

"I challenge."

"Too bad for you. Look. Look out there."

"That's a horse."

"No, it's not. It's a llama."

"What's a llama look like?"

"Like a horse, except it's got more fur. Just like that one."

"I want to be It," Hector said. "You always get to be It. Why can't I be It?"

Helena could see "Wzzat" going down the drain unless she let him have a chance, so she said, "Close your eyes. There's a school with an H-bomb cloud coming out of it."

"I challenge."

He opened his eyes. "You win," she said. "I told the truth about the school but not about the H-bomb part. Now it's your turn."

She closed her eyes tightly this time. She didn't have to cheat in order to beat her brother at anything.

"There's a bird," he said.

"I don't challenge that."

"There's a dead person."

"Where?" She looked around.

"Out there." He pointed to a man painting his house.

"He's not dead."

"He could be."

"He *could* be, but he isn't, you idiot. He's painting his house!"

"Mom! Helena's yelling at me."

Their mother glanced into the backseat and then put her hand over her face.

"Dead people can't paint their houses. If they're dead they can't do anything. So I challenged you and I won."

"He was a zombie," Hector said. "He was wearing zombie clothes."

"What're those?" she asked, mildly interested.

"Black shirts and tennis shoes."

"All right," she said. "I'm It. It's my turn. He wasn't a zombie and he wasn't dead. Close your eyes." Hector followed her instructions, as he usually did. He was such a chump she could only feel contempt for him, although she could remember loving him, when he was a baby and she could hold him. That was before he learned to talk.

She saw a billboard.

MYSTERY SPOT!!!

???VIOLATES THE FORCE OF GRAVITY!!!

VISITED BY THOUSANDS!!! BAFFLES SCIENTISTS!!!

BRING THE KIDS. THEY'LL LOVE MYSTERY SPOT!

RESTROOMS. ¼ MILE

"There's a place with no gravity," she said.

"I challenge."

"Well, it's *there*." She pointed at the roadside attraction. "You go in there and you float up to the sky or something. Dad," she shouted, "how do they do that?"

"It's a tourist trap," their father said.

"So I win," Helena said.

"I'm getting bored with this," Hector told her, slumping down.

"One more." She saw a dead possum in the middle of the highway. "There's a wedding cake, right in the center of this freeway, and we just hit part of it."

"I challenge. I didn't hear us hitting anything."

"Oh yeah? Turn around and look." She pointed at the back window, at where they had just been. "See that white?"

"That's not a cake. That's dead. It's not in our lane."

"A cake is dead. Anyway, we hit it," she lied, "so when we stop next, there'll be frosting on the bumper, and you can taste it, if you want to."

"All right."

Fifteen minutes later, they pulled into a rest stop. Their father limped off toward the rest rooms, and their mother got out of the car to stretch. Helena and Hector jumped out of the backseat and walked up to the front of the car, an old green Chevy Malibu. On the bumper, there were several dead insects, and, on one side, a small narrow streak of dry white residue.

"What're those bugs?" Hector asked.

"Cake decorations."

"Do they taste good?"

"Sure."

"Eat one then," he said.

"Not now. See that white over there?"

Her brother nodded.

"That's frosting from the cake. Taste it."

"Are you sure?"

"Sure I'm sure. Go ahead, Hector. Taste it."

He put his finger down, touched some of the white on the fender, spun around twice, took a finger out of his mouth, and said, "That's nice. It's sweet."

"Huh?" Without thinking, she put her finger on the bumper and then touched her tongue to that finger. It tasted terrible, like garbage or tuna casserole.

"I didn't taste it! I didn't taste it! I didn't taste it! I didn't taste it!" Hector screamed with glee. "*You just tasted bird poop!*" he yelled. He ran off toward the water fountain.

The thing was, it *had* looked a little like frosting, for just a second. She hadn't been totally fooled. Or maybe she had been, and it was the first time her brother had ever done it. He'd never manage to do it again, though. He was a boy, and he would stay stupid forever.

Pawnshop

MADISON SMARTT BELL

I am not happy to see Polo come in because it's hard enough to hear already, with the traffic crunching and munching across Broadway just past the window gates, and the trains slamming down onto the el track off the bridge from Manhattan. KCR is just about to start their weekend Coltrane festival, and I am twiddling my finger on the pause button, hoping to eliminate the dumber commentary, hoping to catch something I don't have already. *Bing!* goes the doorbell, and there's Polo. You can walk right in this place, I don't have a buzzer on the door. Don't need one since I put me and the merchandise behind one of those four-inch Plexiglas walls like they have at the bank and the post office. There's a little shiver down my back as the door slaps shut and Polo comes up toward the barrier in his broken-legged lope.

He's not the reason, though, it's the Coltrane Quartet, and not a bad choice to kick off the program. "Favorite Things."

"Ay, Abe," Polo says, something between a mumble and a slur. "Watchoo lemme habbonis?" His fingers dip into the belly pocket of his filthy sweatshirt and come out laced with fine gold chains. They swing back and forth a little because his hand is shaking, almost in time to the music, not quite. So far, they're playing the tune almost straight. The little gold diddly-bops hanging off the chains look like Elsa Peretti. Polo has been to Manhattan, I think.

"Nothing," I say just trying to listen. . . . With his other hand, Polo snaps up the short brim of the last of his trademark hats, too ripped and grungy for him to sell now or even give away. One of those flimsy little bicycle caps that he always used to claim was a polo hat, which was all he knew, and how come people gave him the name.

"Ease off, Ike," Polo says. "S'real gold here. Hunnud cart. . . ."

"Where'd you get'm?"

Polo smiles, the muscle movement jerking his whole head to one side. "Same way, Izzy, fell offa backa truck, you know." His eyes are the wrong color. I can see he's pretty sick.

"All right." He's ruining the music for me, but I'll still have the tape. "Let's have a look."

And with ferocious concentration Polo manages to insert the chains into the slot above the countertop. There's three of them, look like they go together. I push them around with a fingertip, lining up the breaks. Wonder what happened to the neck they were on?

"No sale."

"Ass gold, Hymie, you *know* ass real gold." This is a little game of Polo's, making up different Jewish names for me. I am as Jewish as he is a polo player. I hold the chains up and give them a shake.

"Sure, but the weight of the ornament, see, is not enough to break the chain. So it didn't fall off the back of a truck. Not possible." And I push the whole clump of chains back through the slot.

"Eh, Zeke, ainchoo go let me back?" I don't answer this one. It's an awkward situation. I did used to let Polo back behind the counter. When it wasn't busy, we'd play chess—you'd be surprised how good he was. I even bought stuff off him sometimes then—only stuff that came in boxes though. I would go watch him in the Golden Gloves. In those days, just to see him walk across the room was like listening to poetry, but then—*crack*— it was all over. Not so long ago, either, only about six months. Now Polo looks like somebody took one of those wire cheese slicers and shaved about ninety percent of him off. What a terrific drug, if only I had invented it I could live in Trump Tower instead of Bedford Avenue. Or maybe I could even be dead, who knows?

"Come on, Ike," Polo says, repeating himself already. He shifts uneasily from foot to foot, anxious as the first man on the sun. Just as an experiment I see if I can make him disappear by changing the focus on my eyes. There's a nice big pothole just outside my shop windows and it can be fun to watch the cars smash into it when they're coming fast enough. I can hear the music again now, they're just starting to blow the lid off the tune. That spot where the piano solo ends and Coltrane takes it back on the third bar of the chorus. There's certain harmonic maneuvers that will take me where I want to go, he said, and sometimes I get impatient and play them all at once. Coltrane on soprano sax. I had one here for a little while. Tried it two days and nothing happened, then finally a sound like the death cry of the last mastodon on earth. So I sold the sucker, at a loss. It was broken, see? It didn't work.

Polo's shadow is still waving back and forth across the windows like seaweed floating in a current, like one of those skeletons that rise up from the grave to offer you a dance. Can't let him behind the counter anymore. He's not trustworthy. What he's waving at me now is a fake Rolleiflex watch.

"Where'd you get it?" I hear myself say, and wonder why I bother.

"Felloffabackatruck," Polo says.

"In our time," I say, "things don't anymore fall off the back of trucks. Doesn't happen. You need to get a new line, Polo. Or take the old one somewhere else."

"I thought we friends, Hymie," Polo says. The solo just goes on and on, less and less imaginable with every note, and I always wonder what he could have been thinking about at times like that—how his feet hurt, sweet potato pie, problems and complexities of living inside the skin he was given—or maybe just nothing at all. I can't imagine what it would be like, to hold that moment in your mouth and feel it flutter there. . . . Polo looks a little yellower than he should, though maybe it's just the scratches or the thickness of the Plexiglas.

"We used to be," I said, telling the truth, by accident maybe. "Still are enough I can't give you money for what I know you'll spend it on."

"At?" Polo says, smiling like he thinks he's got an angle now. "At, man, I give up that bad old stuff, I give it up today."

"It would take a miracle," I say.

"*Look*," Polo says, and waves his arm, and is visited by a flash of pure serendipity, because just at the place where he happens to point, a bakery van hammers down into the pothole, the door flies up, and out pops an enormous wedding cake, to land bang where the dotted line used to be when there was one. I watch a motorcycle swerve to avoid it, and the next thing I know I'm standing on the sidewalk next to Polo looking down at this mysterious object. People are coming out of the bodega across the street and starting to laugh and chatter and point, but except for that it's totally quiet. The cake looks dingy in the dim light that filters down from the el track, but it really isn't damaged much. It's a big one, almost chest-high. The layers have all slipped out of alignment, so it looks like the Leaning Tower of Pisa, and the teensy figurines on top have skidded up to lean against the rim of braided icing, like tourists peering down over a balcony.

"There you go," Polo says. "What more do you want?"

This seems like a fair enough question to me. Already I've got my left hand in my left pocket, spooling a bill around my index finger to give to Polo in a minute—wouldn't do to show him the whole roll. Like I'd lost a bet, though there wasn't one.

Icy Wires

BEVERLY GOODRUM

Early that morning, Alice had heard on the radio that ordinary table salt would work on icy steps and sidewalks. Stepping out in her bathrobe and loafers, she'd tossed handfuls onto the stairs. Children were already playing in the streets.

She was waiting by the door with her packed bags when Eben pulled up to the curb. He crunched right across the smooth front yard and came up the steps, testing each one with his toe. "It's all right," Alice said. "I salted them for you." She could tell by the look on his face that something was wrong.

"Let's ride out for some breakfast," he said, blowing into his red hands.

"We're not going, are we?" She followed him across the yard, shuffling through his lumpy tracks. His car was running on the side of the road, blowing out clouds of gray smoke. When she got in, she saw the black coat hanging flat against the back window, draped in yellowing plastic. The car smelled like mothballs.

"We're not going to New York, are we?"

Eben frowned, adjusting knobs—defrost, windshield wipers, radio. He scrubbed at the window with his fist as they inched down the road.

"There's nothing I could do." Wet drops of snow slapped against the windshield. "Adelia's aunt died. Her favorite aunt."

Adelia was his wife's name. Alice couldn't stand the way he said it out loud. "What if my favorite aunt had just died too? Then which funeral would you go to?"

"You have one aunt and you hate her."

"Well, what if it was my grandmother? Send some flowers."

"Alice, don't be ridiculous." He wiped at the window. "I'm a pallbearer."

"Are you going to wear that?" She turned and hit at the coat's sleeve. She could see Eben in his black suit eating lemon tarts in some kitchen, telling old women he barely knew how very sorry he was.

He leaned over the steering wheel, trying to see out. "I'm as disappointed as you are." The windshield wipers spread the snow in a thin layer across the glass.

No two snowflakes are ever alike, her grandmother used to say, but Alice later learned in science class that this had never been proven.

In town, the stoplights were still blinking yellow as they had since midnight. "Eben, are you going to leave her or not?"

"This isn't the time to talk."

"It's never the time to talk." She breathed gray patches onto the window. "Can you turn the heat down?"

"We'll go someplace next weekend."

"I called in sick this weekend."

Eben gripped the steering wheel.

"Will you button her black dress in the back?"

"No."

"Will you bring her a Kleenex?"

"No." Eben backed into a parking space. He turned off the ignition and turned to Alice. "Yes. Yes, I might. It means nothing. I'd give a stranger a Kleenex."

"Where will you sleep? In the room she had as a kid? What color is it?"

"Goddammit!" He hit the steering wheel with the palms of his hands.

She stepped out into a pile of dirty snow and slammed the door shut.

"Please," he said, following her into the diner. "I'm sorry."

She slipped into a booth and grabbed a menu from behind the napkin holder. She read out loud, "Spaghetti, meat loaf, creamed spinach, home fries, cherry cobbler."

Eben pressed his foot against hers and leaned across the table. His lashes, wet with snow, circled his eyes in little spikes. "Next weekend. We'll go someplace. Someplace we've never been." He ran a finger across the back of her hand. "Someplace you've never seen."

Alice stood at the window. He would be crossing the state line into Delaware about now. There were small footsteps winding across her backyard. Next door, the children were pushing snow into shapeless piles.

They had drunk their coffee in silence. On the way home from the diner, she had asked him to drop her off at the corner. He said he'd call from Delaware and she said, "Don't bother." A corner of the drycleaner's plastic billowed and caught in the door when she slammed it shut. "Don't call ever again," she said as he turned onto the road.

The children were now slapping the piles of snow, smoothing out thick walls. The younger ones, zipped up in pastel snowsuits, were catching snow on their tongues. At recess, her teacher Miss Spader used to say, you can catch snow on your tongue. But remember, frostbite stings and in the end is a dangerous thing.

Maybe he hadn't left yet. She wanted to tell him not to bother calling from Delaware, not to call again. Let him think about that while he carried his corner of his wife's dead aunt.

She punched out the numbers: 563-2334. The phone rang and rang. Usually, if his wife answered, Alice hung up. If Eben answered, he'd pretend not to know her and say things like "Sure, fine, two o'clock, I'll need to check my calendar."

She set the phone back in the cradle and rinsed out her coffee cup. In the yard next door, two boys were breaking tree limbs, snapping twigs, peeling off the bark. Three other children were digging at their icy wall, collecting snow and shaping it into balls. They hurled the snowballs and crouched down. The two boys ran up with their tree limbs—pow, pow. They gunned down their opponents, who crumpled obligingly into the snow.

Once, in April, Miss Spader had invited a police officer to the classroom. He said, who wants to come up and touch my badge? Me, me, me, Alice said, her arm stretched as far as it would go. In front of the class she had touched his badge, but the points weren't sharp the way she thought they would be and she wished she'd waited to touch the gun. She went back to her seat, everyone hissing, what was it like? From the other end of the playground, the children on free recess were yelling rat-a-tat-tat-tat-bang-kill. Under the window, Miss Collins's class stalked in their usual circle, duck, duck, duck, goose. The policeman's badge glittered while he spoke: Never, never, never take candy from strangers.

Alice picked up the phone and dialed 563-2334. She hung up before it rang. She called her office. She designed brochures for a small advertising company. Katy answered. She and Alice were good friends, although they always disagreed on borders. Alice told her about Eben.

"The swine," Katy said.

Alice told her that the whole stinking thing was over.

"Like the other six times." Katy laughed, and for a minute was silent. "You missed it today," she said. "We had to design a sign for doctors. Get this. The poster said, 'Hello, I'm Mr. Penis.' They asked for an expressive face on the tip. They said we could leave off the nose, they said play around with it, use your discretion."

"I'd leave off the nose," Alice said. She wound the cord around her finger. "But listen, this is different."

"Good, I'll tell Brad. He asked about you," Katy said. "Come to the party tonight."

"Katy, do you really think Eben's a swine?"

She pulled on a turtleneck and laced up her boots. She'd ask Brad to take her for a ride in his sports car. He had taken her out to dinner once and he talked all evening about his plan to open his own business, selling streamlined plastic desk organizers. He trimmed the fat from his meat and slid it to the rim of his plate with a knife. His family, he constantly reminded her, had real estate in Nebraska.

Outside the children were yelling. She jerked the newspaper from the table and laid it out on the linoleum so she could wipe her feet when she came back. On the way to the grocery, she'd decide what to make for the party.

They were throwing their snowballs up into the trees. The boy with an orange toboggan threw one high up into the oak. It hit a twig that cracked and fell. A bird flew up from the branches, hovering, batting its wings. The children jumped back, laughing and cheering.

The road had been cleared and the cars, still fitted with chains, clanked across the asphalt. She wished she'd told Eben that she knew about that black suit in the back of his car, knew that he'd worn it at his wedding.

She'd first seen Eben behind a podium, where he was giving a lecture at the university. He talked about some Greek guy, Simeon Stylites, who stood on one leg, balanced on a column, for thirty years. She dug through her purse for a pen and wrote his words down on the back of her deposit slips. She stayed afterwards to ask questions, and when everyone had cleared the auditorium, she and Eben went out for coffee.

The birds perched on the icy wires. Alice tried now to remember the point about Simeon Stylites.

Walking around the corner, she saw what looked like a dead rooster in the middle of the road. As she neared the bus stop, she saw that it was a cake. An elaborate cake, with collapsed plastic figurines. A bride and groom. A wedding cake. When she had once asked Eben about his wedding, he said he hadn't had a wedding cake, that he didn't believe in them. He had a sit-down dinner with rare roast beef. And the dinner, really, hadn't meant a thing.

The icing was smeared on the pavement, but a couple of pink swirled rosettes survived on top of the cake. Snow fell on their sugar tips.

"It's a shame," she said to the man who had come up beside her.

"It's hard to get around," he said. "But I like it. I grew up in Maine."

"I mean the cake."

She stepped up to the side of the road and looked again at the cake. There was a groom, his black tuxedo painted onto the pink plastic body. And a ballerina. Ballerina? The pointed toe touched the knee of the extended leg and thin bare arms arched over its head, posed as if it had been stopped in the middle of a pirouette. The bus pulled around the corner. Alice stepped back to the curb.

She took the first seat on the bus, and leaned her head against the cold pane. . . . Eenie, meenie, mynie, mo. Me me me. Step on a crack, break your mother's back. . . . Tootsie roll, licorice, pumpkin pie, Cinderella, dressed in yellow, went upstairs. . . . The bus pulls up to the curb and splatters people in fancy coats, fox furs with clever eyes. Eben, in his black suit, steps onto the bus.

On the edge of town, the bus jerked along the residential streets. Lights shone from the houses in town and smoke snaked out of chimneys.

In October, Alice had stayed late at the office to work on a brochure for "The Holiday Tour of Homes." When she was finished, Eben had picked her up and driven her home. He sipped coffee to stay alert and she held it when he changed lanes. Lights burned in the windows of the houses above the highway.

"We could be happy like those people on the hill," she had said.

"Happy?" He crushed his cup and tossed it onto the floor. "They're filling out tax forms, skimming dead goldfish from the bowl, picking their noses in bed."

"You're sick," she said and eased her head into his lap, and he put a warm hand on her stomach, up under her shirt.

"Eben."

"What?"

"Why don't you leave her next month?" His thigh had tensed under her head. She slid to the other side of the car.

She pulled the cord and got off in front of the bank. She walked a block and went into the Goodwill thrift shop. Large purple tags dangled everywhere. Couches had tags: Do Not Sit. A piano had a sign: Do Not Play. The saxophone said: "See manager in back room."

She walked down the aisles. She picked up a green gun and pulled the trigger. She wound up a little fuzzy dog. It twirled around and around chasing its tail, then slowed, wobbled, fell over on the shelf.

At the back of the store, in a dimly lit hall, was a phone.

"Call Bruce for a good time: 865-5692." She put a quarter in the slot and punched out the numbers: 563-2334. The phone rang.

"You son of a bitch," she said.

The phone rang and rang.

A lady with a little boy was waiting for the phone. She leaned against the wall holding a plastic dish drainer and a gold belt. The little boy had dark circles under his eyes like his mother. He stood close to the wall, his face an inch from the graffiti.

The phone rang and rang. "Hello," Alice said into the receiver, staring back at the woman. "How about chicken for dinner? You know I hate veal."

"Lady."

The phone rang and rang.

"What about cake?" She turned her back to the woman, and faced the wall. "With icing. Decorations." Ballerinas?

"Lady, this is a public phone." Alice turned to her and frowned.

The little boy traced the letters with his fingers. "Jesus loves you. Eat shit and die. Fuck you." He said each word out loud. He stuck his tongue out and touched it to the red words on the wall.

The woman whacked him. "You don't know what kind of people have been here."

"Fuck you," Alice said into the receiver and hung up. She dug for a pencil and scrawled: "For a good time, call 563-2334."

The last time she tried to end it, he kept calling. When the phone rang she left the house. She spent a couple of nights with Katy. Her mother called the phone company.

Then she had seen Eben downtown, standing in front of a display window at Talheimer's, watching the mechanized badgers and weasels dressed in children's nightwear. They ended up checking into a hotel a block away. They had made love until the sheets loosened and exposed the rough mattress. The street-lights came on and Eben's skin looked pale in the dim light. "I have to go," he said, rising up on his elbow. She pushed him down and began counting the wet hairs flattened to his stomach, lifting each one with a fingernail.

Alice stopped at the grocery for avocados and lemons. Once, she had stopped by the store with Eben. "Wait here," he said. "I'm just going to pick up dog food." To save time, he had said, although she knew he was afraid to risk being seen with her. While he was in the store, she went through the glove compartment. There was a map of Connecticut, a pouch of pipe tobacco, Kleenexes. She found a little bottle of purple nail polish. She unscrewed the top and sniffed it. She brushed some across one nail. When Eben came back out with the dog food, he said, What's that funny smell? She shook a finger at him and said, "Dammit to hell, you son of a bitch, what took you so long?"

It was almost dark when she got home. At the sink, she slit the avocados into perfect halves, scooped out the pits, mashed the green pulp against the side of the bowl until it squeezed up through the tines of the fork. She thought about how things would be without Eben—the way she thought about being old, or dead, or legless.

When she was a kid, she had ways to get through things. She turned her mother into a witch who chained her to the sink and forced her to scrub dishes. When she told Eben about the witch, he said he always thought of the bathtub as the bowels of a giant. In third grade, he learned the Dewey Decimal System and looked up cannibals in the card catalog.

She took the avocado pits and skin outside to the garbage. The children had gone in; their fort remained, icy and hard.

In the quietness, she heard a bird. It sang out loudly, like birds in summer. She spotted it hopping around a fallen branch. Alice approached it slowly, pausing as each foot sank into the crusted snow. It hopped in circles. Beside the branch was a snowball, frozen and solid, as large as a grapefruit. She stooped, near enough to touch the bird. It lifted one wing. The other one clung to its side, the jagged feathers crooked across its body. Alice tightened her hands around it and carried it inside.

She found a box to put it in and called the vet. He told her how to make a formula and feed it with an eyedropper. When she brought the dropper towards the bird, it turned, crying out, twisting its head away. She called the vet to tell him, but the phone rang and rang.

She dressed for the party. But when she was ready, the bird cried out again. She flipped on the television.

Brad called from the party. She said she'd be there soon.

She tried to feed the bird again. It turned its head. She forgot to ask the vet if she should force it.

She ate guacamole from the bowl and watched *Donna Reed*. She dozed off. When she woke up again, the TV was buzzing and jagged lines shot across the screen. She flipped it off. The house was quiet. The radiator kicked. She knew the bird was dead. She glanced into the box. Its body was rising up and down, with even breaths.

The night train whistled its warning. If Eben were here, she'd wake him up, she'd put her cold feet against his legs. He'd jerk, and open his eyes. He'd stare at her, as if he'd forgotten where he was. Then he'd pull her close, folding his arms around her.

The train flew through the night, carrying people far from home. She thought of Eben in Delaware. Her life extended out before her like those metal tracks, and listening to that train whipping down them, she thought about how things would be from now on. She slept again and dreamed of Eben in a black suit. He stood beside a grave, and a bird with a woman's face flew down on his shoulder.

The sun filled the room early, waking her. She was listening for the bird when the phone rang.

"Alice?" It was Eben. Cars and sirens were in the background. She saw Eben in the phone booth, counting out coins, closed in by four greasy rectangles of glass.

"I have to feed the bird." She glanced into the box. "Don't call again." She hung up and unplugged the phone.

She knelt on the floor and touched a finger to the bird's head. The bird flinched slightly. She pressed the dropper against its beak, parting it with the tip. Its neck expanded a little as the warm liquid passed down. She ran a finger along its back. The bird tilted its head and opened its mouth. She let two drops fall.

In the kitchen, Alice warmed more formula. Icicles hung down from the window. The walls of the children's fort had been knocked down, and their snowballs, beneath the surface, appeared as dim holes. Black birds hopped, pecking crumbs of the cookies they'd eaten. They moved over the shell of snow, effortlessly. Then, as if a snowball had been hurled in their midst, they flew up in the air, like bullets shot into space. Above the fort, the birds perched on the icy wires.

Alice imagined Eben stepping out of the telephone booth, and into the street, rushing between cars, yelling—"jerk, assholes" —yelling even as he reached the curb and approached the gas station attendant to get his dollars changed into coins. She knew that if Eben had been with her the day before at the bus stop, he would have ventured into the street to examine the cake. When the light traffic subsided, he would have walked to the center line, knelt on the asphalt to prod the icing with his finger. He would have picked the figurines from the mess, brushed them off, and put the ballerina in one pocket and the groom in the other. And from time to time, when he stepped into a phone booth to call her and dug frantically in his pocket for coins, he would remember them. He'd touch the groom's cold slick body. He'd touch the ballerina's sharp pointed toes, wrap his fingers around her plastic body. Alice knew that he would never wonder why the groom had stood beside a ballerina or why she was posed as if she were endlessly turning. After he deposited the coins in the phone, he would forget about the figures. Eben could carry them in his pocket forever.

A Kind of Flying

RON CARLSON

By our wedding day, Brady had heard the word *luck* two hundred times. Everybody had advice, especially her sister Linda, who claimed to be *"wise to me."* Linda had wisdom. She was two years older and had wisely married a serviceman, Butch Kistle-burg, whose status as a GI in the army guaranteed *them* a life of travel and adventure. *They* were going to see the world. If Brady married me, Linda told everybody, she would see nothing but the inside of my carpet store.

Linda didn't like my plans for the ceremony. She thought that letting my best man, Bobby Thorson, sing "El Paso" was a dia-bolical mistake. " 'El Paso,' " she said. "Why would you sing that at a wedding in Steven's Point, Wisconsin?" I told her:

because I liked the song, because it was a love song, and because there *wasn't* a song called "Steven's Point."

What raised *all* the stakes was *what* Brady did with the cake. She was a photographer even then and had had a show that spring in the Steven's Point Art Barn, a hilarious series of eye tricks that everyone thought were double exposures: toy soldiers patrolling bathroom sinks and cowboys in refrigerators. Her family was pleased by what they saw as a useful hobby, but the exhibition of photographs had generally confused them.

When Brady picked up the wedding cake the morning we were to be wed, it stunned her, just the size of it made her grab her camera. She and Linda had taken Clover Lane, by the Gee place, and Brady pictured it all: the cake in the foreground and the church in the background, side by side.

When Brady pulled over near the cottonwoods a quarter mile from the church, Linda was not amused. She stayed in the car. Brady set the wedding cake in the middle of the road, backed up forty feet, lay down on the hardtop there, and in the rangefinder she saw the image she wanted: the bride and groom on top of the three-tiered cake looking like they were about to step over onto the roof of the First Congregational Church. We still have the photograph. And when you see it, you always hear the next part of the story.

Linda screamed as two crows, who had been browsing the fenceline, wheeled down and fell upon the cake, amazed to find the sweetest thing in the history of Clover Lane, and before Brady could run forward and prevent it, she saw the groom plucked from his footing, ankle-deep in frosting, and rise—in the beak of the shiny black bird—up into the June-blue sky.

"Man oh man," Linda said that day to Brady. "That is a bad deal. That," she said, squinting at the two crows, who were drifting across Old Man Gee's alfalfa, one of them with the groom in his beak, "is a definite message." Then Linda, who had no surplus affection for me, went on to say several other things which Brady has been good enough, all these years, to keep to herself.

When Bobby Thorson and I reached the church, Linda came out as we were unloading his guitar and said smugly, "Glen, we're missing the groom."

Someone called the bakery, but it was too late for a replacement, almost one o'clock. I dug through Brady's car and found some of her guys: an Indian from Fort Apache with his hatchet raised in a nonmatrimonial gesture; the Mummy, a translucent yellow; a kneeling green soldier, his eye to his rifle; and a little blue frogman with movable arms and legs. I was getting married in fifteen minutes.

The ceremony was rich. Linda read some Emily Dickinson; my brother read some Robert Service; and then Bobby Thorson sang "El Paso," a song about the intensities of love and a song which seemed to bewilder much of the congregation.

When Brady came up the aisle on her father's arm, she looked like an angel, her face blanched by seriousness and—I found out later—fear of evil omens. At the altar she whispered to me, "Do you believe in symbols?" Thinking she was referring to the rings, I said, "Of course, more than ever!" Her face nearly broke. I can still see her mouth quiver.

Linda didn't let up. During the reception when we were cutting the cake, Brady lifted the frogman from the top and Linda grabbed her hand: "Don't you ever lick frosting from any man's feet."

I wanted to say, "They're flippers, Linda," but I held my tongue.

That was twenty years ago this week. So much has happened. We now have three boys who are good boys, but who—I expect—will not go into the carpet business. Brady is finished with her new book, *Obelisks*, which took her around the world twice. She's a wry woman with a sense of humor as long as a country road. Whenever she sees any bird winging away, she says to me: There you go.

We're having a big family party here in Steven's Point. Butch and Linda and their brood are coming north for a couple of weeks. Butch has done well; he's a lieutenant colonel. He's stationed at Fort Bliss and they all seem to like El Paso.

People find out you're married for twenty years, they ask advice. What would I know? For years I laid carpet so my wife could be a photographer, and now she'll be a photographer so I can retire and coach baseball.

It's quiet in the store today. I can count sparrows on the wire across the road. My advice! Just get married. It's not life on a cake. It's a bird taking your head in his beak and you walk the sky. It's marriage. Sometimes it pinches like a bird's mouth, but it's definitely flying, it's definitely a kind of flying.

Something Sweet and Wild

PAM HOUSTON

Under the second full moon this December, the high Uinta Mountains look like God touched them. Deep snow covers everything, four or five feet of it. Michael and I live in the high country, but we're headed even higher, to the heart of the Uintas, the highest mountains in the state. We're coming up the canyon from Kamas. There's plenty of snow on the old road, but it's passable, even in two-wheel drive. We're in one of those transition zones, where the canyons meet the mountains and all the rocky formations that line the roadway seem suggestive and weird. Every time we pass a new shape on the horizon I tell Michael its Indian legend: the dancing brave, the mother and child, the three old men standing on the steps to heaven. These legends

96

are entirely my own invention, but if Michael suspects this, he doesn't let on.

It's important to me to go out someplace wild every full moon, and Michael goes along with it, the way he does with most of my ideas. But tonight is New Year's Eve, and even more important, it's the blue moon, the first one in many months, many years even. And I feel that anything might happen under it, given half the chance.

The trees are taller now around us, and the road narrows. A rabbit, brightest white in the headlights, darts in front of us and then runs back, the way it came. Two weeks ago, on a trip to the Grand Canyon, I convinced Michael that the jackalopes he saw on the postcards in Mexican Hat were real. He comes from another part of the world where *Playboy* magazines are illegal and wild animals outnumber people, and no one has ever thought to send a picture of a rabbit with antlers on its head through the mail. Michael's not stupid, and it wasn't easy to convince him. I had to invent a strange mating ritual that made the antlers an evolutionary necessity, I had to make up a hunting season, and imagine a burrow with an entrance a foot or more wide.

"No antlers," he says, after the rabbit has disappeared.

"It's the wrong time of year," I say. "They shed them in the autumn, after they mate, like the elk."

Michael is honest and handsome and affectionate and free. He has been traveling for nearly ten years, essentially alone, looking for something; sometimes he calls it a career. All things considered, his story is not so different from mine. He landed in my town three months ago, and even though we haven't talked about it, there is something to be reckoned with between us. It is powerful and healthy, and terrifying, and though *longevity* is not a word I feel comfortable with, there is something here that, despite our histories, will *last*.

The road switchbacks up a ridge, and I shift the truck into low gear and suddenly we are facing back the way we have come, towards Timpanogos, the sleeping princess.

"See that big snowfield on her chest," I say to Michael. "The one down and to the left of the peak?" Michael turns down the tape player.

"When that snowfield melts into the shape of a horse's head, it's time for the people in the valleys to plant their corn."

Michael smiles at me and squeezes my hand. I don't know where my stories come from. Sometimes I just open my mouth, and there they are.

Michael turns the tape player back up. He listens to the corniest music of any human being I have ever known. We're talking Gordon Lightfoot, we're talking Andrew Lloyd Webber show tunes. The first time I ever got in his car, John Denver and Julio Iglesias were singing a duet called "Perhaps Love," and Michael was singing along, operatically, with Julio's lines.

Now Sarah Brightman is singing "I Don't Know How to Love Him," and a deer steps into the path of the truck near the head of the canyon. A doe, alone, taking advantage of the moonlight. The truck makes no sound as the brakes lock up on the snowy road and the doe leaps over the guardrail and disappears into the forest. The truck spins 360 degrees and then rights itself. I pull to the side and Michael gets out and locks the hubs. I slow down considerably after that. The snow on the road is getting deeper.

"Do you know what it means when a deer crosses your path from east to west in the moonlight?" I say.

He shakes my hand back and forth to let me know he doesn't know. "It means there is great happiness ahead for you," I tell him. "It means there are good things to come."

I have a meadow in mind that I want to ski to, a place where I want it to become midnight, a place where I want us to drink our champagne. But I've never been up this road this deep into winter, and by the looks of it, no one else has either. I'm not sure how far we'll get.

Two full moons ago we went to Zion. During the day we hiked to Angel's Landing and I took Michael's picture, a close-up with my big lens. When I picked it up at the photo store it stood out among the photos of Zion's red-and-orange monoliths like some kind of an icon amid ruins. There's a look he has for me that I caught in that picture, a look that is desire and seduction and love too, but that's only part of it. The look is a question that demands an answer, some opening of me that is frightening and deep and unknown: an underwater cave, a minefield, a prayer. When I'm at my strongest I can meet that look and even return it. Most times, though, I have to look away. When I paid for the pictures I said to the girl behind the counter, "This is the man I'm going to marry." Swear to God. I've never said that before in my life.

We've made it to the trail head, but I'm afraid to stop the truck without turning it around first, so I hit the brakes and we do another 180. We're in the middle of the road and the snow is at the running boards, but it's downhill all the way home and there won't be anyone else who wants to get by tonight.

Outside the car, it is cold and crystalline. We add clothing and wax our skis. Michael has borrowed boots that are heavy and way too big for him. Here we are still below treeline, but soon we will ski up and almost above it, and we will see the whole mountain range, all the valleys, lit up and shining under this rare blue moon.

We are only a few hundred yards down the trail when a tremendous flapping of wings makes me freeze and three great gray owls lift off the ground and into the air. I slow down and let Michael get about fifty feet ahead of me. He and I are synchronized in these wild places instinctively, like wolves who bump shoulders and know what it means. To talk would be redundant. This is one of the best things we have together; it's the thing we had together before we ever met.

Michael is skiing along in front of me, shuffling really, with his poles in one hand and the champagne bottle in the other. Over sweaters, he's wearing the leather fringe jacket I bought him for Christmas, and a cotton fishing cap that says *Victoria Falls*. He comes from a place where it is never cold, but to look at him tonight, you'd think he grew up on these mountains.

He stops for a moment, and lets me catch up, then loudly and in Tswana, the language of the country where he's been working most recently, he says, "I am filled with the joys of living," which I recognize because he says it often, and because it sounds like the names of three or four of Santa's reindeer spoken quickly, without breaths in between.

My instincts tell me Michael feels the same way I do. But other, more familiar voices inside me say no. Unconditional love is so strange to those of us who aren't used to it, we keep trying to rename it, to give it another motive: malice, dishonesty, pain. It's like driving a car in a foreign country; there's always that instant where you find yourself wanting to turn onto the wrong side of the road.

Michael brings home movies from the video store and we watch them: *The Sound of Music*, *An Officer and a Gentleman*, *The Man from Snowy River*, *Crocodile Dundee*. In all of his favorites—in every single rental he brings home to me—the movie never ends when the hero finds his career.

We are out of the heavy trees now, and the snow sparkles diamonds on all sides of us, hundreds of thousands of them, the way I remember fireflies in summer back East. It is cold if you don't keep moving, so we do, toward the meadow I remember, acres of untracked powder set between the last of the ponderosas and a cliff face to the west. To the east, there's a view farther up into the heart of the mountains.

We get there just before midnight, pop the cork on the champagne, and despite the cold, despite the snow that is everywhere and bottomless, we make love. And after, when Michael is lying on top of me, kissing me hard and trying to wrap me inside his coat's warmth, twelve gunshots shatter the air far, far down in the valley. Midnight. New Year's.

"Someone lives down there?" Michael says.

"Someone might," I say, "but it could be the ghost of Taylor Brown." I take a deep breath. "Taylor Brown settled that valley over a hundred years ago, looking for silver and animal pelts. No one knows what happened to him, whether one of his mines caved in, or a grizzly bear got him, or if the solitude drove him so crazy he just wandered off into the woods. All they knew down in Kamas is that one spring he didn't come down the mountain for supplies."

"And now?" Michael says.

"Well," I say, "that was 1902. And in the winter of 1903, and all the winters since—only when it gets very, very, cold, and only under the full moon—some of the townspeople hear gunshots, sometimes way up on the mountain, sometimes down very close to town, and they all swear it is Taylor Brown's blackpowder rifle. Did that sound like a black-powder rifle to you?" I wait for his answer, but incredibly, here at nine thousand feet and five or six degrees above zero, Michael has fallen asleep.

He is not a quiet sleeper. All night, even at home in bed, his mouth is moving, and his hands, just lightly on me, play a very soft song. It used to keep me awake for hours, but now I've gotten used to it, like a train whistle that comes every night at the same time.

It is so silent here, and I'm not too cold yet, but I'm afraid to let Michael sleep, afraid I'll fall asleep too and we'll freeze here together, so I shake him awake and he jumps like a deer.

"You take me to all the best places," he says, and I smile. He says, "If only I was big enough to hold all this loveliness."

Over and over he takes my face in his hands and tells me the truth, and all I ever have for him are stories.

We shake the snow from our clothes and drink the rest of the champagne. On the long ski back to the car, Michael plays what he calls Don Quixote Man of La Mancha with his ski poles and the trees. He shouts something that his accent and the distance disguises, then I hear the thwack of the ski pole, and then the softer sound of snow falling on snow from the limbs of the tree. I would like him to kiss me again, I would like to know if we made the gunfire, but I don't ask. I am too scared to say I want anything from him, and the reason is simple: if I say I want one thing, I'll have to admit I want it all.

We get back to the place where the owls were, and again, we disturb their hunting.

"Do you know what it means when three owls cross your path twice in one night in the moonlight?"

"What?" he says.

"That you are blessed by Little Bear," I say, "first assistant to the goddess of love." But this is as close as I will come. Even here, in the snow and under the blue moon, I will never come closer than this.

At the car he kisses me again and I wait for the sound of gunfire but this time it doesn't come. The moonlight lets me read his expression. It is different from the way he usually looks, tender, and not without sadness, but there is also something sweet and wild.

Then we notice that we have left our hats in the meadow.

Michael offers to go back for them, but he's already told me his heel is bleeding from the borrowed ski boots, so I go instead. I ski fast, silently, past the owls without waking them, and when I get back to the meadow, the moon has moved. Soon it will be behind the face of the cliff. I see our hats lying in the single snow angel our bodies have made. For now the snow still sparkles in moonlight, and I can see coyote tracks, fresh ones that have gone to the place where the hats are, investigated, and moved on. I look at the place where the tracks disappear into the ponderosas.

"What does it mean when a coyote crosses your ski tracks?" I say to the meadow.

The wind moves the branches slightly, and the moon slips behind the cliff. In the sudden darkness, there is no answer at all.

I ski back toward the truck, back toward what's left of the moonlight, and when I get there I see that Michael has been building something in the snow. At first I think it's a snowman, but when I get closer I see that it's a wedding cake, three-tiered, almost as tall as me, and he's built it right in the middle of the snowy road. He's decorated it elaborately: small pine boughs ring each tier as garlands, shiny stones dot the top of each layer, two pine cones stand side by side on the very top under a canopy of twigs.

The car is closed up and warming, but through the door and over the engine I can hear Christopher Plummer and Julie Andrews sing, "But somewhere in my youth or childhood . . ."

"It's an old Eskimo custom," Michael says. "The husband-to-be builds a wedding cake out of snow, and the day the last bit of it melts back to the earth, he knows it is time to wed."

Michael stands close to me without touching. I breathe in the night and the cold runs crazy and clear through my brain. He gives me the Zion look and this time I return it.

I say, "Michael, marry me, please."

Eternally Yours

JOY WILLIAMS

In the beginning, it wasn't much of a road. That was the nicest thing about it.

The wedding cake in the middle of it was made of molded plastic. The cake was pretty, all right, but it was made of plastic. Plastic cakes had become the custom. People would have the real cake at their weddings, something small and tasty, just big enough so that everyone could have a little piece, and then they would have the fake cake, something outrageously showy and big, something that wouldn't make a mess if a child accidentally bumped into it in the reception line and sent it clattering to the floor. The real cake was real, of course, and its tendency was to disappear. The false cake was super-real and being made of plastic would stay around forever. This particular cake, this first cake that appeared in the middle of the road, was seven tiers tall and wide as a compact car. It wasn't chocolate with white icing. It didn't have layers of carrot, raspberry, pistachio, or double lemon creme. It was made of heavy-duty, durable super-gloss white plastic that would last and last and last long after the road which had started out being nothing much turned into a six-lane highway, long after the big trees had been cut down and burned, long after the bride and groom who had pitched it out along with the artificial Christmas tree had passed away, on and out.

Ashes to ashes and dust to dust, they used to say, but this was before modern times. Now the wedding cake had become eternal. It did not discolor, chip, or disintegrate. It did not age or weather. It did not rot or molt. It was inedible and indestructible and offered neither home nor nourishment for anything or anybody. And it was so large and shiny that no one ever ran over it. Birds and beasts fared less well on the highway. They perished quite consistently against radiator grilles and beneath tires, but people would slow and go out of their way to avoid hitting the wedding cake in the middle of the road. Partly, this was because they were a little superstitious about it, but mostly it could be very damaging to their vehicle to hit an object of such durable and heavy-duty plastic. Even the huge trucks that sped by in the middle of the night filled with drums of toxic waste—the color within of a shade not found in nature—even these hardened and laconic truckers who spoke only with others of their kind (and toward the end, they were an elite and growing number) did not run over the wedding cake in the middle of the road.

No one knows who actually dumped the first wedding cake there. They were desperate people, perhaps, at wit's end. Or perhaps they were just dumpers. They had to dump the thing somewhere. And it became the place where everyone brought their plastic wedding cake, used that once for display on their wedding day. No one wanted to use someone else's plastic cake. And who would want a used one when new plastic wedding cakes, hundreds and hundreds of them, were being made daily? So this was where they ended up, in this highly specialized dump.

All dumps had become, by then, highly specialized. One dump would accept only cars, another only unfashionable kitchens and bathrooms. The dumps became as big as towns, ringing the so-called real towns where people lived. People made excursions to these places, for there were scarcely any other excursions to make. And they were certainly conveniently close by. The dumps were renamed parks, the old concept of parks as a place of trees and wild things being outdated. Some of these parks were nicer than others, of course. No one wanted to go to the Toxic Dump Park or Fast Food Container Park. Bottle Dump Park was fairly popular, particularly at sunset when the dying light made the broken glass sparkle. The very nicest was Wedding Cake Park—known as THE PRETTIEST PLACE PLASTIC EVER MADE. Plastics are not tapped into the secrets of things; their molecular structure makes a hidden life impossible and they have no secrets to share. The wind moved around the plastic cakes in silence. It was a silent place. Still, people went there right up until the end. They kept marrying and wanting cakes right up until the end. They were hopeful, in their fashion, until the end. And the wedding cakes jumbled together in a big, frothy, white, hard heap upon a barren and befouled plain were there. Until the end.

The Wedding Cake
in the Middle of the Book

KELLY CHERRY

It was white cake with white icing. There were tiers of it, layers stacked like a ziggurat or Mayan ruin, so that if you had been very small, the size of a clothespin, say, and light enough on your feet not to sink into the frosting, you could have climbed from the bottom to the top. You would have encountered pink sugar roses with green mint leaves, and curlicues of the white icing that looked somewhat like tracks or skid marks in snow. You might have thought that someone had been skating on the icing, doing figure eights and crossovers, and gliding along in a straight line around and around. And there are worse ways to spend one's days, you might have thought, than drawing a straight line in a circle. On the second layer, there were white swans, probably of marzipan, floating on a lake made from a pocket mirror. As they swam, they could see their reflections, like Narcissus. A ballerina in a white tulle skirt and satin bodice danced *en pointe* at the edge of the lake, her stretched neck repeating the pattern of the swans' necks, one arm arched over her sculpted head, one extended like a wing. If you had wanted to, you could have watched for a while; you could have stayed to the end and applauded, applauded not only for her graceful, complex performance but for the long-ago days she had reminded you of, when you, too, were poised for the curtain to rise, on your own life, which, you thought, would surely be graceful but which had only been complex. Another tier, and there were tiny white dogwood trees, all in flower, the blossoms bearing the narrative of the cross all around the lacy edge of the cake. Buttery butterflies slept dreamlessly in the dogwood branches, occasionally fluttering, as if about to wake, and causing a blossom or two to break off. Blossoms kept falling off and drifting to the layer below, suspended for a moment on Swan Lake and then sinking to the bottom of the mirror. Perhaps these blossoms had been fashioned from Tic-Tacs. The penultimate tier was rather celestial, with white clouds of sugar wafers. Sometimes it snowed, and then confectionary flakes fell on the dogwoods in bloom, and on the butterflies hidden in the branches, and on the dancing girl and swimming swans, and on the fiercely single-minded ice skater, who went on gliding, even while snow covered up his tracks. At the very top of the cake there were two figures, one male and one female, both about the size of clothespins. They were groom and bride, and wanting to wish them well, you would surely have gone up to them—*Best wishes go to the bride, congratulations to the groom!*—and you would have been so surprised, then, seeing them close up, to realize that they were your parents on their wedding day, your mother brilliant in her stern beauty, your father naively handsome in his early twenties. They were there at the top of the cake, waiting for you, waiting for you from the beginning of time—if you had been as small as a clothespin, and able to climb a cake without making a mess of it. You could have looked into their faces and seen what they saw, or what they failed to see. You would have been able to see the world before its creation. And then you would have wished them well, because that was what you had always, always, always meant to do, and you would have descended again, through blizzards and springtime and music and the astonishing facts of intention and determination, and when you leapt off the last mysterious ledge, like a leap of faith, like leaping from a Babylonian or Mayan mystery into the light of day, and landed at the bottom, what you would have seen, which you could not have seen before, was that on one side of where you were the road ran north, and on the other side south—or maybe it was east and west—and all along the way there were trees, and houses, and telephone poles, and people going places and coming back from them.

The Trial

GREGORY McDONALD

"The wot in the middle of the road?"

"The wedding cake, Your Honor."

"Oh, I see."

His Honor did not see the relevance of a wedding cake in the middle of the road to his courtroom, to whatever it was that was under discussion there, to the world at large and whatever was going on out there.

What His Honor did see was that Mrs. Butterfield had taken, from the Bench's point of view, the seat which best showed off the shape of the lady's, in this case Mrs. Butterfield's, calves. The seat Mrs. Butterfield had so cleverly chosen was at the right front corner of the balcony, in front of the floor-to-ceiling arched window. Thus, said calves were gloriously backlit. The light not only held said calves in splendid silhouette, it also erotically softened the lady's Supp-Hose.

His Honor muttered, "Damned clever of her. Damned nice of her, too, I must say."

"Beg pardon, Your Honor?"

His Honor glared at the dandy Prosecutor's dandy tie decorated with pink impatiens on a blue background. "Damn well you should."

The criminal Clerk of Court asked, "Do you mean that remark to be taken down as a part of the permanent record, Your Honor?"

His Honor grinned at Mrs. Butterfield. "Why not?" His Honor was not opposed to the *beau geste*, the *petit geste*, or even the silly jest. Life, he recently had been advised by the Judicial Retirement Board, was short.

"I wish to remind the Prosecutor, this is an informal inquest to determine if a crime has been committed, if so, what category of crime, and who, if anybody, is to be bound over accused of that crime for trial by jury."

His Honor always had felt on firm ground uttering *parole* from the bench. It saved him from having to hear things. Now, he knew, he must exercise restraint in his remarks. The Judicial Retirement Board had made some comments regarding his increasing garrulousness in court, which comments His Honor hadn't quite caught in their entirety. Something about his remarks from the bench averaging seventy-three percent of all oral utterances in his recent trials.

His Honor treated himself to another glance at the calves of Mrs. Butterfield. He hoped his glance at the balcony would be taken by all present in the courtroom (except Mrs. Butterfield) as an appeal for patience. "Get on with it."

"Yes, Your Honor. We intend to prove, without a question of doubt, that with malice aforethought, cold-blooded premeditation, the accused, Gary Keeler, did, in fact, contrive circumstances which resulted in the death, the murder, of Ms. Maybelle Mayhew."

His Honor leaned over and inspected the exhibition table in front of the bench. He had been holding gas entirely too long.

"And what is the alleged lethal weapon?" His Honor asked.

"A wedding cake, Your Honor."

"The devil, you say."

"No, Your Honor: a wedding cake."

"Sounds too mushy to me. And where is this alleged lethal weapon?" His Honor craned forward again. At dinner just the night before he had mentioned to Mrs. Butterfield his suspicion that his increased flatulence was caused, at least partly, by the imported mineral water she was ordering him by the bottle. The Judge had noticed that the better restaurants had never served him bourbon or rye by the bottle, but they did mineral water, as if it was something they were determined to get rid of at any violation of taste.

"It did not hold up as an exhibit, Your Honor," the Prosecutor said softly.

"What's that? Speak up."

"The wedding cake. We have only a few crumbs left, Your Honor, in that plastic bag in front of you, marked Exhibit A."

"Ah." With that survey of the exhibit table, His Honor was certain he had exported every last gaseous bubble of the mineral water. "Sounds a crumby lethal weapon to me."

"Be that as it may, Your Honor."

Defense stood and orated at considerable length regarding the innocence of the nice-looking young man whose murderous intentions the dandy Prosecutor, the Judge supposed, previously had decried.

The defendant, His Honor noticed, had brown curly hair, wide-set eyes, jutting jaw, broad shoulders, and a flat stomach probably never expanded by expensive imported gas. Clearly, that young man, whatever his alleged crimes, had never had to drink gas to increase any woman's ardor for him.

His Honor was glad Mrs. Butterfield could see little of this male exhibit. The Judge did not want Mrs. Butterfield's memory jogged by What Might Have Been and Probably Was. In his campaign to get Mrs. Butterfield between the sheets, His Honor suspected he surely would suffer by comparison with the accused.

Defense was a heavy man, with a colored shirt, gray suit, and brown shoes. Even as a student the Judge had noticed that those of his classmates who were going into Criminal Defense always belonged to the mix-and-match school. The legal theory behind this choice of apparel, the Judge understood, was the belief that a sloppy appearance was perceived as democratic and therefore of appeal to the average jury composed of twelve uncomfortable, begrudging, bored, and therefore sloppy citizens.

Prosecuting attorneys naturally took the other tack, of appealing to the judge in any case by dressing as nicely as they assumed the judge dressed, as, after all, they were paid by the same source, watered at the same well, as it were, the People. Representatives of the People were expected to dress well, although, of course, the People didn't, as, by and large, they couldn't afford to, having to work a quarter of the year to pay the clothing bills of their representatives.

Of course few knew what the judge actually wore under his robes behind his bench. For all anyone but his clerk knew, a judge might only be wearing a dickey, clip-on tie, and athletic supporter.

One of the benefits of being hard of hearing was that His Honor was not only free to, he was obliged to allow his mind to wander as the attorneys for both sides went through the formalities of presenting their evidence.

His Honor caught some of what Defense was saying: the excused might be a beef, and was repaired to testicle to that erect, but surely not a herderer . . . had never afeared in tort afore . . . despite his how admitted transmissions, had felt the same yob in the clock womb of the same apartment more for six tears . . . sincerely lubbed the diseased, was engaged to worry her, and did intend to worry her . . . had, in feed, bought the wedding rake and did not defy he had met said wedding flake in the muddle of the hoad, that he was wordly indulging in the lubful lobhay of the argent hooter . . .

His Honor had decided that if he ever succeeded in getting Mrs. Butterfield between the sheets, then, and only then, would his he hoped resurrected self-esteem permit him to purchase and use a hearing aid for each of his ears. Over the years, His Honor knew his ears had been damaged greatly by evidence. Only then would he be able to return the haughty looks of the Judicial Retirement Board and admit to a hearing difficulty without feeling he thus was admitting a more general incompetence.

As Defense's opening statement wore on, His Honor saw no reason for not indulging himself in a concentrated survey of Mrs. Butterfield's calves. Years on the bench had taught the judge that with a sufficiently concentrated expression on his face, he could indulge himself by look, thought, and even deed in any silly thing he wished. During the trial of that serial killer, whose name His Honor could never remember, Scott Simone or something, he had read the entire works of Stephen King. During a somewhat shorter trial, of a sheriff accused of having his fingers in an illegal bingo operation, His Honor had tried his own hand at writing an improbable. He was just getting to the part in his story where the sexy judge discovered that the X-ray vision prompted by having been hit on the head by a golf ball could be used to serve his dispensing justice in court by allowing him to perceive everyone's genetic predisposition to false utterances by the shades of gray in certain brain cells when the trial ended, despite his best efforts to prolong it to the completion of the final chapter. Throughout the trial, scribbling at his bench, he had been pretending to be taking notes. In the trial, which cost the state two million, three hundred and fifty-six thousand dollars and forty-eight cents, the jury found the sheriff guilty. Always mindful that power corrupts, the Judge sentenced the sheriff to a full week's probation. The clerk, who believed he was doing a good thing, and probably was, having believed His Honor really had been taking notes all that time on the bench during the trial, threw said notes away. Except for the odd letter of argument to his credit card companies drafted on the bench, the Judge never again attempted creative literature. However, seeing that Mrs. Butterfield had placed herself in the courtroom so knowingly, so cleverly, so kindly . . .

Defense, believing His Honor was casting his eyes upward and to the right in another divine appeal for patience, concluded his opening remarks ("I abjure you, Harry Feeler is in a vent!" or so the Judge heard) and sat down.

A few moments passed before His Honor realized that nothing whatsoever was transpiring in his courtroom. His Honor never minded such pauses, as he knew he could trust his concentrated expression to be read as reflection.

Finally, the Judge said, "Call your first witness."

His Honor was always glad when witnesses took the stand. They were closer to him. More to the point, in the witness box they were microphoned. He had a fairly good chance of hearing some of what they said.

"Your occupation?" inquired the dandy Prosecutor.

"I drive a milk tank truck."

"A milk tank?" inquired the Judge.

"Tank truck," clarified the Prosecutor.

"Not something intended to mow down cows?"

"No, Your Honor. Something that transports milk."

"Well, yes," His Honor agreed. "A cow does that."

"If you would tell us, sir, what happened the night of March 17th?"

His Honor smiled up at Mrs. Butterfield. The Judge remembered what happened the night of March 17th. He and Mrs. Butterfield had met at the green beer bar at a St. Patrick's Day dance.

Coyly, in the balcony, Mrs. Butterfield returned His Honor's smile.

She, too, remembered.

". . . no way I could avoid it," the driver said.

"Avoid what?" His Honor asked.

"The wedding cake."

"The wedding cake . . ."

"It was foggy!" the driver declaimed. "I was barrelin' along at exactly the speed limit, no plus or minus, travelin' at a safe speed, you understand, for the fog, and there it was, in the middle of the road!"

"Where was this?" the Judge asked.

"Outside Edwardsville."

"Outside Edwardsville is many places," the Prosecutor said. "Tell the Judge exactly where you were."

"Comin' down that little road just north of Edwardsville, down the side of the mountain, you know, along the edge of the cliff, just a little bit beyond that cottage other side of the road! There's never nothin' on that road at night!"

"But on the night of March 17th there was something on that road," the Prosecutor encouraged.

"Suddenly, loomin' up at me outta the fog!"

His Honor liked the milk tank driver as a witness very much. His every word was shouted.

"What was?" His Honor asked.

"The wedding cake!"

"A looming wedding cake?" His Honor shook his head. "How does one get a wedding cake to loom?"

"A trick of the light, Your Honor," the Prosecutor offered. "Doubtless Your Honor has noticed that in a fog things are apt to appear a good deal bigger than they are."

The Judge nodded. That certainly had been true of Mrs. Butterfield that very same night.

"Objection!" Defense shouted. "My fraternal brother in the law is instructing the court!"

"Overruled."

"I braked!" the driver insisted. "I couldn't believe it! Fourteen years drivin' a milk truck and I never hit a wedding cake in the middle of the road before, not once!"

"Serendipity," His Honor remarked.

Mrs. Butterfield smiled down upon him. Often she had remarked that their meeting that same night over the green beer had been serendipitous.

"The coming together of the cake and the milk, I mean," His Honor amplified.

Meaning to keep the demeanor of the court, he shot Mrs. Butterfield only a quick smile. The rest of the court doubtless thought His Honor had suffered a twinge.

"Then I saw the headlights! Down in the gully at the bottom of the cliff! I knew there was no way a car should be down there 'less it went off the cliff!"

"So what did you do next?"

"I couldn't climb down there! No way! I stopped in Edwards-ville and called the cops!"

Defense had no questions.

However, His Honor did ask the milk truck driver, "Are you married?"

The driver answered, "You think I'm crazy? With a good job like mine?"

Next witness was the police officer who was the first to arrive at the scene of the alleged accident.

"On the road," the policeman asserted, "was a smushed wedding cake. The milk truck hit it, all right, I guess. Really smushed it."

"How did you get down the cliff?" the Prosecutor asked.

"Rolled."

"You rolled what?" His Honor asked.

"Myself, Judge. I tripped near the top. And rolled. All the way down. Rolled and rolled. Over and over. It hurt somethin' fierce. Bruised my chin." The officer of the peace, having mentioned it, touched his chin. "My elbows." He established by touch which parts of his anatomy were elbows. "My knees." Locale of his knees was established merely by look. He put his hand behind his back . . .

"Yes," the Prosecutor interrupted. "And what did you find at the bottom of the cliff?"

"Miss Maybelle Mayhew. And her car all scrunched up. I guess as the car rolled down the cliff, a door broke off. Maybe she was trying to get out. Anyhow, I'd say on the car's last roll the frame landed on her and squished her out like a tick. I mean, all her considerable insides had been squirted all over the place, onto the bushes . . ."

"That will do, Officer."

His Honor said, "Squirted, eh?" He made a note. His Honor had not entirely abandoned his wish to try his hand at a novel, if ever he could curb his clerk of his tidy instincts. " 'All over the place, onto the bushes . . .' "

"Deader'n a Christmas tree on the Fourth of July."

"And did you recognize the deceased?" asked the Prosecutor.

"Sure. Who wouldn't recognize that broad?"

"Did she have distinguishing features?"

"Yeah. Like I just said: broad. She weighed over three hundred pounds if an ounce. Her wig had fallen off, but I recognized her even with her white hair. She hadn't clipped her mustache off over her lips lately, but I recognized her all right."

His Honor looked at the handsome young man at the defendant's table. He was engaged to a woman weighing over three hundred pounds? With white hair under a wig? With a mustache that fell over her lips?

His Honor wouldn't have thought it of him.

"What was the deceased's name?" the Judge inquired.

"Ms. Maybelle Mayhew, Judge," the policeman answered.

"Well, at least she was born to be pretty," His Honor said mildly.

"She lived in that cottage just at the top of the cliff," the policeman volunteered.

Defense had no questions.

Next witness was the manager of the local department store.

"We had tried Ms. Mayhew as a salesperson at several counters, perfume, lingerie, shoes. We even tried her in sports, thinking she could heft the dumbbells easily enough. In every department she served, sales fell to zero. Apparently customers objected to the slight spray which emanated at them through her mustache when she spoke. Finally, we put her in the stockroom with the other hardies."

"And is that where the defendant, Gary Keeler, worked?" asked the Prosecutor.

"He did," the manager responded curtly. "He no longer does."

Defense had no questions.

Next witness was a weeping telephone operator.

What the Judge heard her say was "I taught Smary hoved we."

His Honor handed the operator a box of tissue he kept for just such occasions under his desk. "Do dry up."

"I thought Gary loved me" was the statement that finally came through harshly air-blown pipes. "Then he told me he was engaged to marry up with that Mayhew mountain."

"And did the defendant, Gary Keeler, give you any explanation for his change of heart?" asked the Prosecutor.

"Finally," acknowledged the witness. "He said Mayhew was blackmailing him into marriage. She had caught him one Sunday selling things he had stolen from the department store's stockroom on the sidewalk in St. Dismas. Mostly electronic entertainment things, clock radios, VCRs, little TVs, toasters. He said he was stealin' and sellin' to keep me in diet pills. Maybelle said if he didn't marry her, she'd report him. He'd lose his job. Get arrested. Be sent to jail for Grand Theft Toasters, or somethin' terrible."

Defense had no questions.

"Defense calls only one witness, Your Honor," was announced by Mix-and-Match as he rose from his table. "Gary Keeler."

"Oh, dear, no," said His Honor. "I'd prefer Mr. Keeler to stay where he is."

The clerk looked up at His Honor. "Judge . . ."

His Honor glowered at the murderer of literary ambitions. "Oh, all right."

As the handsome young defendant mounted the witness box, turned around facing the courtroom, and sat, His Honor sat on the bench as straight as he could, stretched his shoulders, and expanded his chest under his robe.

Nevertheless, he could see new light in the face of Mrs. Butterfield in the balcony as she leaned forward to study the curly hair and smooth cheeks of the alleged first degree murderer in the box.

"Damn," muttered His Honor. "There go my hearing aids."

The clerk, unpunished murderer that he was, whispered, "But you don't use hearing aids, Your Honor."

"Wot?"

In a deep, mellifluous voice, the accused testified. "Maybelle was crazy to have this enormous wedding cake, ordered and made special, five tiers high, all white curlicued frosting, formal dressed bride and groom standing on top, all lovey-dovey. When it was ready, March 17th, she sent me for it. So I called her saying I had picked it up in St. Dismas and invited her to meet me in the pub in Edwardsville."

"There's a pub in Edwardsville?" inquired the Judge. "Any good?"

"Only I thought I'd surprise her. Before I called her, I put the big wedding cake in the middle of the road near her driveway just down the hill toward Edwardsville. She had said she couldn't wait to see it. So I guess in her hurry she came out of her driveway in the fog, saw the wedding cake in the middle of the road, swerved to miss it, and drove herself over the cliff."

The attractive accused smiled beguilingly at His Honor.

The Prosecutor had questions. "Are you a thief?"

Defense: "The accused is not being tried as a thief in this court."

Accused: "Sure."

Prosecutor: "Was Ms. Maybelle Mayhew blackmailing you?"

Defense: "The Prosecutor must present his own evidence on this matter, Your Honor."

Accused: "Sure was."

"Defense rests, Your Honor."

In the balcony, Mrs. Butterfield's eyes never left the accused as he returned to the defense table with springy step.

After a moment of silence, the clerk asked, "Would you like to retire to chambers, Your Honor?"

"I'd like to retire to that pub in Edwardsville."

"Well, then, what is your finding, Your Honor?" the clerk asked.

"I find against the milk tank driver."

"The milk tank driver? He wasn't accused."

"He's the one who smushed the wedding cake, isn't he?"

"Your Honor," the dandy Prosecutor beseeched. "I beseech the court that the accused, Gary Keeler, be charged with first degree murder and be bound over for trial by jury."

"Nonsense," said His Honor.

The dandy Prosecutor's dandy eyebrows shot toward his hairline. " 'Nonsense'?"

In the balcony, Mrs. Butterfield was leaning over the rail, her eyes on the accused.

"In this matter of State versus Keeler," intoned the Judge. "Two people drove down that foggy road that night." He cleared his throat. He raised his voice. "The night of March 17th. The first, the deceased, Ms. Maybelle Mayhew, saw the wedding cake in the middle of the road, and so great were her ambitions to marry the accused, she drove herself over the cliff to avoid smushing the wedding cake. The second, the milk tank driver, saw the same wedding cake in the middle of the same road, and not similarly driven by marital ambition, drove right over it, thus smushing said wedding cake." His Honor raised his voice if not to the heavens at least to the balcony, where Mrs. Butterfield hung over the rail attending the accused, not the Judge. "This court can only conclude that the deceased, Ms. Maybelle Mayhew, was driven by her own lust to fling herself over the cliff. Her lust, and only her lust," His Honor fairly screamed, "for an attractive man much younger than herself precipitated her actions which resulted in her own grisly, undoubtedly painful demise."

Still standing, dandy eyebrows nudging his widow's peak, the Prosecutor asked, "Your Honor, is that your considered opinion?"

"It is." His Honor looked at the figure hunched over the balcony rail. "All things considered."

Picture Perfect

ANN BEATTIE

The stylist clips the barrette half an inch higher in the bride's hair. Her curls could be sun-struck water, pouring down a waterfall. It crashes just above her lovely shoulders. The neckline of the dress has been altered to reveal the hollow area at the base of her neck where her clavicle bones meet. The bodice is sewn with seed pearls. Shoulder pads, though not as exaggerated as in previous seasons, puff her shoulders into an approximation of angel wings.

The second roll of thirty-six is in the photographer's pocket. The sun isn't strong enough and the frustration isn't yet great enough to explain the photographer's anxiety, but suddenly he's removing his cap, dabbing his forehead with the Irish linen handkerchief from the previous day's shoot. He makes an unconscious moue as the bride puckers her lips so the makeup artist can wield the lip brush to redefine one corner. The photographer's assistant is out today because last night he won a strawberry-eating contest, and by morning was covered with hives.

This business is harder than people know. They do know it isn't glamorous—name the profession that is—but they might not expect the lengths people will go to to get the right shot.

For instance, the wedding cake. The wedding cake was created especially for this shot. Though the baker, Monsieur Antoine Huppert, presented the stylist with a leather-bound book containing both 8 × 10 black-and-white and Polaroid color pictures of twenty wedding cakes he could produce, none was considered perfect. Cake 15 came closest, but was too frou-frou as the icing was piped into flowers where the ribbon swirls tapered down on the sides. A day was spent with Monsieur Huppert at the National Gallery of Art, where he was asked to consider some aspects of Flemish floral still lifes to loosen up his style. Altered cake 15 met with the client's instant approval.

Today, that cake is present only for reference: an ongoing, inspirational off-camera deity, of sorts. There is Monsieur Huppert's original cake, and then its double and triplicate—those altered and fortified with shaving cream and porcelain flowers hand-painted to look like real calla lilies. It would have been madness to have only one wedding cake. What if bugs flew into the frosting? Or if something truly disastrous happened: a meltdown, when the sun was full. It was Monsieur Huppert's pleasure to make two backup wedding cakes. Sculpting with Colgate shaving cream was a fascinating experience. He has been paid more, for his time and effort, than if he had made two hundred wedding cakes.

But imagine this: the photograph is not being taken to advertise a wedding cake, or even a bridal dress. It is being taken to illustrate the concept: *Disk brakes are highly effective.* The thankful and astonished bride has run out into the driveway/road to see that her car has stopped short of crashing into her wedding cake. This scenario is meant to illustrate the bride's anxiety that things will go wrong, be out of place—that somehow chaos will prevail. Wouldn't it be the bride's nightmare that the wedding cake was, inexplicably, in the middle of the road? And without her disk brakes, she would have run it down! Some symbolic road kill that would have been, on the way to church. Better to flatten Gerald Groundhog or Peter Possum than the Three-Tiered Triumph.

Clouds pass overhead, and the photographer dabs at his forehead again.

"You know why calla lilies are so popular these days?" the stylist says to the bride.

"Don't make her talk," the makeup artist says.

"Why?" the bride says, hardly moving her mouth.

"Because this is the era of public speaking. They look at those flowers, and they think it could be their moment in the sun. Calla lilies look like microphones."

"We're waiting for the clouds to pass. Let's keep it together, folks," the photographer says.

"How many times have you been married?" the stylist asks the makeup artist.

"Three times," she says. "Don't remind me."

"I would love to be out of this underwired brassiere," the bride says. "I would just love love love it."

The photographer moves from behind the camera. He takes a light reading from the bride's cheekbone. He moves the light meter down a foot, checking the reading off the front of her dress.

The clouds get grayer. A wind begins to blow.

"This will be it, folks," the photographer says. "If it rains today, this will be the day I retire. If it dares to rain, when we have this rented estate for only one day, if it dares to rain, it will be the absolute end."

Monsieur Huppert shrugs. "They look like real rainclouds to me," he says. "They're translucent, so there's no way somebody launched cardboard cutouts into the sky."

The first raindrop falls. Quickly thereafter, the second. The bride squeals, gathering up her dress and running for cover. The stylist follows behind, holding her train. The makeup artist is so upset her brush falls to the ground. The photographer looks at Monsieur Huppert, as horrified as if someone had opened fire on them with buckshot.

"Up there," Monsieur Huppert says, pointing. "*Quel dommage*: she is crying—the big bride in the sky."

Route 80

DAVID LEAVITT

Josh and I are leaving each other. These last few weeks we've spent together, at "our" house, trying to see what, if anything, could be salvaged from five sometimes good years. At first things went badly; then we started gardening. Josh has always been an avid gardener, while I couldn't tell a lily from a rose. How roughly my vacant acknowledgments of his work rubbed up against all the effort he put in, all those springs and summers of labor and delicacy! And did my not caring about the garden mean I didn't care about him? After he left, naturally, the flowers turned to weeds.

The therapists in our heads told us this was something we could do together, a way beyond talking (which meant, for us, fighting), like the trip my mother and father took to watch the sea elephants mate. Kneeling in the dirt, holding the querulous little buds in their nursery six-packs, there was another language for us to speak with each other, as virgin as the leafy basil plants we patted into the soil; our old, gnarled, tortuous relations were rude and hideous weeds we ripped out by the roots.

I made up dramas as I planted, horticultural B movies in which I was the hero defending the valiant rose from the villainous weed. Or I was the valiant rose, and Josh the villainous weed, and the hero was someone I was hoping I might meet someday. Or I was the villainous weed.

Digging, I came upon little plastic stakes from past seasons, buried deep, unbiodegraded, photographs and descriptions of annuals Josh had planted in more innocent, if not happier, times, and which had long since passed into compost.

There is the top of a wedding cake in our freezer. It is frosted white, and covered with white-, orange-, and peach-colored frosting roses. It was left there by the young couple who sublet the house when Josh and I, unable to decide who should stay and who should go, both went. Jenny and Brian are saving this wedding cake to eat on their first anniversary, which is apparently a tradition for good luck. When I came back, they moved into an apartment where the freezer was too small; the wedding cake stayed behind.

There is a road, too. I don't like roads, the way they run through everyplace on the way to someplace else. The road is where we lose dogs and children, the way we take when we leave each other.

This road, in my mind at least, is Route 80. Josh and I used to say that our lives and destinies were strung out along Route 80, which runs from New York, where we lived for years, to Morristown, New Jersey, where he grew up, to Iowa City, where he went to school, to San Francisco, where I grew up. Even though our house is nowhere near Route 80—and perhaps that was the first mistake—it is Route 80 I imagine when I imagine the wedding cake, like a pie in the face, being thrown.

I was driving along, this long and painfully lovely July day, when I saw the orange lilies spilling from their green sheaths. Until two weeks ago, when I finally asked and Josh told me, I wouldn't have noticed them, and I certainly wouldn't have known they were lilies. Now I know not only lily, but fuchsia, alyssum, nicotiana, dahlia, marigold. Basil needs sun, impatiens loves shade. At night I read tulip catalogs, color by color, easing gradually toward the blackest of them all, Queen of the Night. All of this I have finally let Josh teach me—but (of course, of course) too late.

The lilies shed their petals, at dusk, onto the road. And don't they become, for me, frosting flowers, freezer annuals, with their sly, false promise of good luck? I can feel them smearing under the wheels, sugar and butter, a white streak like guano where a bridegroom is racing away from his bride.

With my parents, going to see the sea elephants became a tradition. Josh and I joined them once. The huge males shimmied along the rocks toward their waiting harems, and the hands of my parents, in spite of all that had passed between them, reached toward each other like flowers reaching toward the sun. My parents' hands were brown; there was dirt under their nails.

Who can claim that our love does not endure, less like flowers than like the little stakes with the photographs of flowers, stubborn beneath the soil?

Perennial.

The Quality of Silence

MARITA GOLDEN

"Public morality is a requirement, private morality an option, don't you think?" Joseph Llwelyn said.

They were discussing a Capitol Hill sex scandal involving a homosexual Congressman, his prostitute lover, and large sums of cash. Buoyed by a new twist on a very old story, the two couples had discussed the tale over appetizers, drinks, and the main course. The friends were the kind of people who always knew what to say. Over dinner they had celebrated the reconciliation of one couple, the impending marriage of the other.

"Oh God, here come the late-day profundities, and he's not even drunk yet," Peter said.

"And the worst part is, he's convinced it's all unique, every word," Meredith said, tossing her red hair as she gave her husband a light peck on the cheek. "Don't you, Aristotle?"

"Surrounded by barbarians on all sides." Joseph sighed. "Come on, Deidre, you're the psychologist. Surely you agree."

"You're the lawyer, Joseph. You have a talent for revealing the self-evident. Who at this table would disagree with you? Not because you're right, but we're your friends."

"Maybe I should just leave now." Joseph faked a rise from the table.

"How'd we get on politics anyway?" Peter asked.

Deidre smiled. "It's always politics when you're more than two seconds with Joseph."

"Hey, I work on the Hill."

"That'd be a great insanity plea if you ever need one," Peter said, handing Joseph a lighter across the table.

Finished with their main course, they sat companionably on the roof of an Italian restaurant near the Capitol. The place was packed. The surprise of a seventy-degree evening in March had brought out the aides, secretaries, and assistants who made Alfredo's a Hill hangout. The feverish gossip about pending legislation, office politics, press leaks, and committee hearings was a verbal rite of passage, a way to slough off the stressful remains of the day.

As Peter's girlfriend, Deidre had met Meredith and Joseph two years ago. Now she sat leaning against her fiancé's arm. Peter squeezed her shoulder frequently, as if to assure himself that she was there. Her hand reached beneath the table, to his thigh.

"You know," Deidre said, "now that I think about it, I get relatively few patients whose problems involve issues of morality—either public or private. Mostly, my clients come to me with broken promises, violated trusts, emotional burdens thrust on them when they were too young to handle them."

"Politicians do much the same thing to unsuspecting voters," Peter said.

"Voters don't *have* the luxury of being unsuspecting anymore," Joseph said.

"I think you're right, Joseph," Deidre said. "But definitions are terribly important in this. Our sense of what's moral and what isn't. Incest and wife beating—in the confines of one's home— aren't considered moral issues by the people who are doing these things."

"Until they're discovered," Meredith added.

Looking closely at each of them, Deidre asked, "When was the last time you even *used* the word 'morality' or 'morals' without a sneer or a sense of embarrassment?"

"What a package," Meredith thought, looking at Deidre Stockton, Washington-born and Yale-educated, with her corn rows and Anne Klein suit. Only a black woman in 1990 could pull off such a contradiction. Meredith studied Deidre's face, as she often did, for some sign of uncertainty that would provide relief. Deidre's eyes were large as small moons. Her face, made up subtly to enhance those eyes, was a declaration. But of what, Meredith did not quite know.

At that moment, Deidre was using her hands, as she often did, like sophisticated, fine-tuned weaponry. When she spoke, pressing her palms together or letting her perfectly manicured nails form a triangle, or resting her hands flat before her on the table, the elegantly cut diamond in her engagement ring sparkled. Once, Meredith had teased Deidre about the way she used her hands. "I've worked hard all my life to be listened to," Deidre had responded. "To be understood. I guess that has something to do with it. Maybe I don't fully trust words alone. They're so easily distorted."

———

"I still say this whole thing is about the Congressman having sex with men instead of women."

"That's a neat summation," Peter said, motioning for the waiter.

"We start out talking about politics and then end up on morality. Isn't a quiet little dinner safe from the onslaught of the monumental?" Meredith was clearly annoyed. "I thought tonight was to celebrate."

"Yes, I've been back home two hundred and sixty hours and thirty-five minutes and six seconds," Joseph announced, checking his watch. "Home to stay," he added with a glance toward Meredith. Abruptly he picked up his beer and finished it, his movements not quite swift enough to hide the resignation in his voice.

"Let's order dessert," Meredith said with strained cheerfulness.

Only recently, Meredith had wrested her husband of twenty-five years from the competent but less experienced grip of a young Senate aide from New Jersey. Joseph had begun an affair with the woman, and then moved in with her after informing Meredith that he wanted a divorce. Meredith had met this demand with a single-minded patience. She lost weight, displayed no rancor or bitterness, and every week invited Joseph to their house for dinner to discuss a "purely business matter," or to lunch, "so that we can at least still be friends." When it was over, she had informed Peter, "All that little bitch had to offer was a twenty-four-inch waist and great sex." To others she said, "I know the man inside out. There was no way she could keep him."

With her thick dark red hair, her drill sergeant's gaze and determined mouth, Meredith was a woman who would simply never allow her husband to leave her.

"And how would you analyze this moment?" Meredith asked Deidre.

"I wouldn't."

The first silence of the evening arrived. And to their surprise, they were all relieved by the unexpected break. Joseph ordered another drink, a double, switching from beer to scotch. Meredith took tiny cautious bites from her chocolate cake.

Twenty-five years. The thought horrified and intrigued Deidre. She and Peter were to marry in June. How many affairs would they be able to survive? How soon would they become bored with one another and publicly abusive, as though even a facade required too much effort?

They had already gone through premarital counseling. Peter had resisted the idea at first, arguing that years of counseling had not saved his sister's marriage. Deidre had countered that they would get help before they needed it, and that there was the racial matter to consider. During the first session she admitted to doubts about whether they could survive other people's prejudices.

"There are issues of credibility in my own community. Racial loyalty," she had said to the counselor. "Also, Peter's parents are quite opposed to our marrying. My parents have gradually come to accept Peter. But Peter's father wrote him a letter saying it was all right to be involved with somebody like me, but that men like Peter didn't marry women like me."

A little later in the session she had said, "We go to parties with Peter's friends who are oh so liberal and have traveled all over the world and speak the right political lines and yet I'm virtually the only black person there and nobody would dare talk about what that means. I love Peter and I know he loves me. But I'm surprised by how much resentment I feel sometimes."

They had gone through almost four difficult months of counseling. She wanted everything out, all the secrets, all the weaknesses that could snare them later. Peter had blown up one evening after a particularly traumatic session. "You treat our relationship as though it's one of your clients, to be analyzed, repaired, and then added to your list of success stories," he raged. "Well, dammit, I'm not a client! I want to marry you. I'm not perfect. I never will be. And I don't necessarily want you or some damned shrink pawing over my emotions like this."

They had met when Peter was covering a convention of black psychologists for his newspaper. Over coffee at the Washington Hilton, he interviewed Deidre about a paper she had delivered on the emotional adjustment of black students on white college campuses.

After discussing her methodology and the significance of her findings, Peter asked where she had gone to school. Deidre described her years at Wayne State in Detroit, where she had graduated a year early, and the rigors of Yale, where the need to prove herself as a black and as a woman had given her a drive that everyone thought came from popping pills. She even found herself describing the mixed feelings of family and friends about her academic success. Her mother, though proud, urged her not to get "too smart."

"I think she just wanted me to remember my place as a woman, the way she'd had to," Deidre said. "She was afraid that the more I knew, the more discontent I felt, the greater the risk I would be for some man to love." And she told him about her minister uncle, who because of her proper-sounding speech, her passion for discussing psychology, had set down his fork during one Thanksgiving dinner and said, "Girl, you been around those white folks too long."

"And what hurt the most, I think," she had told Peter, "was that nobody defended me. Nobody said a word. So, in a sense I was condemned by them all." Embarrassed by the ease of this confession, Deidre suddenly grew brisk and businesslike. "And twenty years later, black students face the same attitudes," she said. "Not much has changed."

When she stopped, Deidre saw that Peter's face was virtually transparent, lit by a blunt, unapologetic desire for her. "White males," she thought, suddenly unable to bear his glance. "What presumption." She finished her coffee and excused herself. She had another symposium to attend.

Peter had never dated a black woman. There were times when he was attracted to the ones he met through his work. The black women who navigated through his world had a profound sense of who they were and where they wanted to go. Their schools and colleges were like the ones he had attended. These women had mastered, he thought, the geography of his universe. He never quesrioned why a similar fluency in their world was not required of him.

His parents were professors at the University of Virginia, his father a noted biologist, his mother a professor of French. Theirs was a form of genteel Southern racism so mannered and fused with paternalism as to inspire in them bouts of self-congratulation whenever they had to state an opinion on "that issue." They were both considering early retirement to work on projects they had not found time for in recent years. But Peter knew that the "unrest" on the university campus was a part of his parents' decision as well.

In the world of Archibald and Jessica Caldwell, "unrest" took in everything from the increasing number of black and Asian students in their classes to the recently formed Nazi Student Union to what they deemed the unseemly debates about the canon. The university, they liked to remind Peter, was to be a citadel of pure learning, untainted by political fads and cultural fashions. "Some ideas are universal and endure," his mother had informed him sweetly. "And we all know in our hearts what those ideas are."

Peter had rebelled by attending U. Mass Boston, despite his parents' disapproval. After graduating, he joined the Peace Corps and served in Liberia for two years, digging wells and teaching illiterate adults to read. In those years he had learned that most of the world beyond America's shores was a mess and that despite the Peace Corps ads, one person rarely made a difference.

When he chose journalism as a career, his parents' regret was deeply felt. They had wanted him to be a scholar and he had chosen to be, in their words, "a journeyman." And yet he loved them. They were his blood.

When Peter called Deidre at her office to check the quotes he had used for the story, he knew he would ask her out. He never allowed himself to consider the possibility that she would say no. And in fact, she didn't.

A year later, he was in love with her, despite the fact that she was maddeningly rigid, and planned even her moments of spontaneity. His cluttered desk, his casual assumption that life would simply turn out all right, astounded Deidre. She bristled with the will to be significant, to live her life as legacy rather than experience. And that was, Peter knew, what drew him to her more than anything else. He found her hunger irresistible.

Dessert revived them. Conversation picked up again. Over coffee they talked of movies, books, the dramatic shifts in the weather. Joseph was blustering and defensive, his voice rimmed with a jagged edge. He and Meredith had clashed when he ordered another drink. As the two men settled the bill, Meredith methodically stroked Joseph's shoulders.

Leaving the restaurant, they walked down the well-lit streets of Capitol Hill. The houses, most of which had once been the property of blacks, now gleamed with the evidence of gentrification. Bay windows, unadorned by shutters or drapes, revealed chandeliers and sleek decor.

Deidre walked beside Peter, holding his hand, their footsteps echoing in the dark. Meredith and Joseph strolled slowly ahead. Once Joseph raised his voice—"Just give me some time, dammit, give me some time!"—and Deidre reflexively moved closer to Peter.

They passed the Library of Congress and the other federal buildings, the ornate dome of the Capitol lit dramatically, looking like nothing so much as a huge white marble wedding cake in the middle of the road. The buildings claimed the night as naturally as the stars overhead. As they neared Union Station, Meredith turned and said, "Let's window-shop a bit."

"Oh no," Joseph groaned.

"Just a few minutes?"

"I'd like that," Deidre said.

Union Station was majestic after an extensive renovation. The great hall with its marble floor and fountain was ringed with stores and shops and looked like an upscale bazaar. They stood for a few minutes taking in the cacophony of good times, a pianist near the fountain accompanying the relentless pursuit of happiness in the restaurants and bars.

The store windows overflowed with objects needed and unnecessary, playful and optional. There were stores that sold only fragrant soaps, stores that sold only socks.

As they stood before a shop that sold art deco ceramics and sculptures, Joseph lost interest. Turning abruptly he collided with a young black teenager. "Watch it, man," the youth said, his tone sharp but jocular. Joseph brushed past the young man, hunching his shoulders defensively. With a shake of his head, he muttered, "Niggers."

The youth stood, clenching his fists, a shallow pool of grief shining in his eyes. He was no more than seventeen, Deidre guessed, his hair cut in a fade, with razor-sharp lines diagonal on both sides of his head. Spotting Deidre, he lanced her with a look of contempt.

"That bastard's crazy," the youth said, meaning Joseph, who now stood in front of a leather-goods store a few feet away. The young man's lips curled as he looked at, then dismissed each of the others. He strode away, stopping twice to look back at Deidre. She felt herself melting beneath his stare.

"Let's get out of here," Peter said. Silent, walking fast, breathless, they hurried to the parking lot. The Capitol building sat in the distance, ahead of them, silent and shimmering in the moon's glow. Once again Deidre thought of wedding cakes—three-tiered, white, untouched, uncut. When they reached their cars, parked side by side, Meredith hugged Peter and Deidre quickly. She whispered, "I don't know what's wrong. I think he had too much to drink." Joseph sat in the car on the passenger side, gazing out the window.

The drive to Deidre's apartment was a long one. Peter tried to pull her closer, but Deidre moved away. When he attempted to talk, Deidre turned on the radio. Twisting the dial off, Peter yelled, "What do you want from me? Just tell me what you want!" Deidre stared ahead in silence.

Once inside her apartment, though, she turned to him in fury. "Why didn't you say something?"

"What was I supposed to do? He had too much to drink."

"That's no excuse. Why didn't either of you say something to him?"

"Say what?"

"That boy was abused. So was I. So were you."

"What could we say?"

"Why couldn't you just acknowledge what happened?"

"Oh, please, don't turn psychologist on me. I don't think I can take it. Not tonight." Peter jerked off his tie and twisted it around his fist.

"I should've let you know, each one of you, right there, how awful what happened was."

"Don't you think we could imagine that?"

"No, I don't."

"That's not fair, Deidre, and you know it's not true. Look," Peter said, "I've got to go. You know I leave for San Francisco in the morning. We'll talk about this when I get back." He paused. "Deidre, I don't want you to confront Joseph and Meredith about this."

"Why not?"

"I'll talk to them."

"I thought they were my friends, too."

"They are. They're good people," Peter insisted.

"The world is full of good people like them."

"Look, I'm sorry about what happened. We all are."

"It must be nice to be white, Peter, to never have to imagine any other reality than your own."

Peter kissed her on the cheek. "I'll call you from California," he said. Deidre was rigid in his arms.

As she sat on the edge of her bed, wrapped in the silk kimono Peter had given her, Deidre realized that she had never been called "nigger" in her life. In the black neighborhoods of her childhood the word was remarkably flexible and resilient. It could be used to deride slovenly, unacceptable behavior or people. And sometimes, when properly decoded, it was a term of affection. But tonight there had been only one meaning.

In the white circles that had shaped her academic and professional life there were other ways to express the word's intent. There had been visible, sometimes audible discomfort when she entered meetings during her internship at New Haven. There were the frequent questions from colleagues about life "in the ghetto." For it was assumed that her blackness made her streetwise and tough despite her polish.

As they had rushed to their cars, words had clogged her throat so that she feared she would be sick. Now, stretched out on her bed, she again felt them rise in a rush. She began to sweat and thought that if she embraced this silence she could not marry Peter. If she broke it, she wasn't sure what he would do.

The clock beside her bed said midnight as she dialed the phone. The phone rang three times. "Hello." It was Meredith's voice, sharp and clear. Deidre's palm was slick with perspiration. The phone nearly slipped from her hand.

"Hello, Meredith."

She wanted to talk to Joseph.

"Deidre dear, we're both so sorry. Joseph feels just awful. You know him—what happened tonight is totally out of character. He didn't mean it."

"What *did* he mean, Meredith? Tell me that!" Deidre shouted.

Later, in the dark and naked in her bed, she again saw the face of the young boy. She could not forget how he had looked at her, or how she had stood mutely inside the shadow Peter and Meredith cast, gazing at the boy as brother and stranger. Deidre removed her engagement ring and laid it beside the clock. She had no idea what she would say to Peter when he returned. She only knew this time she would not let him be silent.

The Time for Love

BHARATI MUKHERJEE

I am in the car easing around earthquake damage in our driveway
and my wife is at the front door waving me off to another July
day overscheduled with edentulous patients.

"Beat me with your shoe!" she shouts. "Go on, do it in front of
the neighbors! Starve me, torment me, break my body into pieces!"

I am not a wife-beater. My vices are gluttony and petulance.
My virtues—equally lusterless—are rectitude and diligence. I
am a hardworking, overly cautious prosthodontist who made it
from Sylhet to Walnut Creek by staying just alert enough to life's
breaks.

"Fatima?" I don't get out of the car.

"Who needs handouts from you?" Fatima screams. "Don't I
have brothers? You like it here, *you* stay!"

A brother's duty is to shelter his abandoned or widowed sisters. She has five brothers. The trouble is that only one of them, a parsimonious pharmacist, still lives in Sylhet. The others have drifted to where the jobs are, to Dubai, to Bahrain and Qatar. Now they're in Amman, repairing automobiles and dreaming of repatriable riches.

"A wife's place is with her husband," I scold.

"In that case," Fatima snaps, "let the husband also buy himself a San Francisco–Dhaka ticket!"

"Fatima, please." I cut the engine. "Talk sense. I can't retire yet."

I am forty-three, and passably healthy. Fatty Ershad, one of two dentists I co-own a medical building with in Oakland, went through a quadruple bypass last week. In the hospital Fatty said, "Old boy, if it doesn't work out, promise me one thing only. Promise me that you'll ship the old carcass back to Sylhet." Fatty's wife, a pert, pretty, convent-educated girl from Mymensingh, ran off two years ago with a housepainter–cum–Buddhist priest. Fatty's lived in Oakland thirty-two years, and still acts a transient.

"You care only about your assets! You don't care about me!" Fatima stands fidgeting in the doorway. Her head and body sheathed sleek in the blue sari she sleeps in, she looks like a beached, baleful mermaid. I should guide her back to tropical seas.

"Please, Fatima. No hysterics."

We are the only Bangladeshi family in an orderly block of landscaped yards and shingled or stucco houses. Neighbors are spying from behind designer blinds. I long for anonymity.

"Let them watch." Fatima plays with the doorknob, but she doesn't go back in. "Let them learn that we people quarrel differently from them."

I should start up the Miata, escape into rush-hour traffic.

"Money isn't everything! People matter! Even wives!"

"You want to go back to Sylhet? What's in Sylhet?"

"Everything."

Her voice, a whip, leaves welts. Once upon a time that voice had wooed me with Kavi Nazrul Islam's poems.

"Keep it soft, Fatima."

"You mistreat me, but that's okay." Even her whisper can sting. "But how about Bibi? Is this any kind of place for bringing up Bibi? You want your daughter to remain chaste or no?"

When my wife says "chaste," you can hear the vicious smack of tongue and palate.

"Bibi's American. You can't ship her here and there like a dead body."

Stay? Or quit? Fatty Ershad made it through. He'll stay on. He'll keep piling up a hard-currency fortune. I want. I want more than money market funds and CDs.

Bibi is ten. My wife would like us to go back to Sylhet before Bibi turns eleven. Eleven, my wife claims, is when girl children in her family mature into women.

"Fatima, what's the hurry?" The Golden State allures and traps. Who can guarantee chastity? "We'll discuss this tonight."

"Discuss this tonight," my wife mimics. She overdoes my assiduously acquired American accent.

My late father would have slipped his stiff-soled leather sandals off his feet and chastised a mocking wife. My loafers are stuck on with Crazy Glue. Maybe I've let go too much. I suffer loss, I yearn for synthesis.

"Discuss, discuss," she goes on, clanking gold bracelets. "You want to expose your own daughter to muggery and rape?"

It is like this with us every morning. The Salvadoran who keeps the yard looking nice for the Goldbergs next door doesn't even look up from his pruning. On our block, every yard except ours is worked on by Salvadorans. They are, Ed Goldberg's explained, mostly undocumented political refugees. His point is that we who've been blessed with more luck or more peacetime in our birthplaces should be hiring those who've had to wetback their way across the Rio Grande. Ed doesn't remember the War of Liberation for Bangladesh; I don't want to remember. Paddy fields swampy with blood, ditches clogged with corpses: in Walnut Creek they seem shameful secrets of an unconventional adolescence. I'd gladly hire Ed's yardman, but Fatima won't hear of squandering savings. "Can we take fancy bushes back to Bangladesh?" She never talks of our not going back; she talks only of how soon we can sell.

"Why exaggerate? People mug and kill in every country."

"Exaggerate!" Bitterness mists her face. "You read the *Chronicle*. You watch CNN. This country's too full of crazinesses!"

"Shut up!" In Fatima's panic, I hear the footfall of addicts, molesters, marauders. Stay or go? Risk or protect? Who can save? I, petty patriarch, thrill to new lusts, dream monstrous dreams. "Just shut up!"

"So sew up my lips!"

Who knows, maybe she is the realist and I the foolish fantasist. She has plans, sensible plans for how to double or triple our savings. We'll take our dollar loot back to Sylhet, buy up paddy fields, set up factories to manufacture denture-base material and make a killing. The pharmacist brother is already scouting factory sites. Thank goodness, she coos nights, we come from an over-populated, cavity-free but plaque-prone country.

Color stability, shock absorption, warp resistance: I hear my wife's incantation. I want to be a dutiful husband and parent. I want to love. Really.

"Fatima," I hear myself say instead, "call a friend. Get someone to drive you to the mall. Go see a movie. Get out of the house."

She winces, as if I've flat-handed her across the face. "Go on," she weeps, "list all my deficiencies. You wanted to marry a modern, convent-educated girl like Mrs. Ershad. Someone you can disco-dance with, someone who speaks English."

My parents picked Fatima as my bride from a short list of four. I never think of the other three. Who needs Fatty Ershad's misery?

Fatima goes on. "You were an America-trained big shot, and look what you got stuck with! Someone who can't drive, can't make friends with . . ."

"You hear me complain about driving?"

Women in Fatima's old-fashioned family are trained to be helpless. She grew up not being allowed to drive, bike, swim, play vigorous games. If femininity is diffidence, Fatima is exquisitely feminine. She needs me. She needs me to chauffeur her places, to punch cash out of ATMs, to work the electronic gadgets in the house, even the small ones like the coffeemaker and the clock-radio. The clock-radio—a gift from the brothers in Amman—is shaped like a mosque and wakes us every morning with a taped muezzin. If I didn't set the alarm, Fatima would remain bed-bound.

"You need to get out of the house."

"Get out of the house?" Fatima mocks me again. "Get out of the house so worse things can happen?"

"Call Mrs. Ershad. Or call Barbara Goldberg, see if she's . . ." I turn the key in the ignition.

Fatima continues her screaming. "Send Bibi and me home! I'll go on a hunger strike if you don't send us home!"

Next door, Ed Goldberg is pulling himself efficiently out of Barbara's hug. He waves to me. Barbara still has an absentminded arm on Ed's left shoulder. Such public displays of conjugal affection used to embarrass me when I first got here. I grew up thinking love was contraband.

"Hi, there," Barbara smiles.

Ed says, "Hot enough for you, Abe?"

Abe for Abdul. Where's the harm? I wave back at Ed. "Never too hot."

Fatima immediately infects our small talk about weather with her belligerence. "Our kind of heat is different. This is dry heat. It is giving burns and headaches. Our heat is wet-wet."

Ed throws her a puzzled look.

"My wife's very sensitive to weather."

"Well, in that case, her garb makes a whole lot of sense."

Fatima, reacting badly to her sari being called a garb, rushes indoors without saying anything more to any of us.

I like Ed. I've tried to convince Fatima that there are good Americans, but she says that if Bibi had been arrested for shoplifting as Ed's daughter was, she'd have hanged herself in shame and that Ed's being so open about his daughter's conviction just goes to show that he, too, lives in a moral vacuum. Ed doesn't worry about losing face as we do, that's my point. He gave us the full story, for instance, of how Shearson Lehman pink-slipped him last March. The company didn't finesse the bad news, he told us. One day he was in Florida on a generous expense account, next day he was unemployed. Fatima and I grew up being secretive about misfortune.

"Hey!" Ed calls out to me, pulling a toad out of his pocket and lobbing it at me as might a magician. "Like this little guy?"

A squishy rubber creature with suction pads on its stomach attaches itself to the front window of my Miata.

"Is it a winner or is it a winner?" He clowns around with a fistful of rubber toads, aiming them at his wife, and the Salvadoran.

I envy Ed his bounceability. I couldn't have gone from managing portfolios to hawking novelty items. This country's full of crazinesses, that's what Fatima'd said. What she doesn't get is that in this country you can cash in on craziness and make yourself a winner.

"Have a nice day!" Barbara says. To Ed. To me, too, I think. Then she goes back into the house.

The Miata cozies me through blocks where well-exercised, well-adjusted families surge in and out of well-kept houses. Children on monsterbikes roar up and down sidewalks. All around me wives are seeing their husbands off to work. Midsummer sunlight is burning off haze, and with it, anxiety, guilt, loneliness. "Beat me with your shoe!" "Have a nice day!" In that sun-gilded air, the commands blend. Toned-bodied temptresses appeal for love. *Yield!* I hear the Miata's subliminal grunts. *Do it! Succumb!*

Near the school grounds, I spot Bibi the Chaste. She is on her way somewhere with her friend Lauren Lepic, and Lauren's mean-looking three-legged dog. Some days the dog wears an artificial leg, but he isn't wearing it today. The dog keeps hopping awkwardly for the Frisbee in Bibi's hand, and Bibi, giggling, keeps pushing the dog away. Bibi is obese, but nimble. Every time she dodges the dog or tosses the Frisbee, her belly—oh, the flesh so salaciously adult, so velvety-naked!—spills over the waistband of her pants and her T-shirt tautens against her chest.

"Dad!" Bibi yells. "Hi! Aren't you late or something?"

"Go home," I order her. "Your mother needs you." Then, voyeur and parent, harrowed by—by what? her near-womanly effulgence? my own imminent prurience?—I pop in the Buddy Holly cassette (Double Playing Time! 23 All-Time Greatest Hits!) that some Miata salesman has left in the glove compartment, and escape to the freeway.

Elvis and Bill Hailey made it to Sylhet, but not Buddy Holly. I didn't grow up on American movies or American rock or American anything. The only American person I ever actually talked to as a schoolboy in Sylhet was a tall, bony WHO doctor who gave us rides in his jeep and who motivated in us a freakish concern for health. Rats were gluttonous, this American explained; they snuck into granaries and gave us famines and plagues. "Guys," he instructed us, "blow 'em away!" He paid us for each rat we killed. We didn't have to drag in whole corpses to collect; tails were enough. The American's plan was to help us help ourselves. What he never caught on to was that we bred rats to protect our bounty-hunting business.

So I am on 1-580, rocking to Buddy Holly or at least trying to, when a semi rams the back of a refrigerated truck on an overpass and sends huge vaporous sides of beef and hog scudding down on the freeway. One moment Buddy's singing, "If you were to say to me today, the time for love is now . . ." and next moment a frozen pork belly's flattening my head.

When I come to, a tow truck's backing into me and an ambulance is pulling away. Cars have arranged themselves in a nasty pile-up. The Miata's totaled, but somehow the thunderbolt of frozen meat has traveled a trajectory of benevolence. I feel beat up, but I'm not on a stretcher. I read the warning: like Fatty Ershad, I must decide if, when the time comes, I wish to be shipped back to Sylhet.

Relief can express itself in embarrassing ways. I realize exactly how embarrassing when the fellow who towed me says, "Just shock, man." I don't look down. I don't have to. My pants feel wet.

From the gas station I call Edith, the office associate I share with two other prosthodontists in Oakland.

"The bozo!" Edith means to console me. "You goin' make him pay?"

"Make whom?"

"You goin' stiff the bozo for pain?"

She's talking litigation, I'm thinking cosmic accident. This isn't the first time we haven't connected.

"I need a favor, Edith."

Edith doesn't laugh when I explain she'll have to take my clothes to Wong's 1-Hour Cleaning in the mall. "Is that in my job description?" is all she says.

I say nothing and, for a while, she says nothing. The phone line picks up other voices. "Abdool?" Edith comes back on the line again. "I'm cool. Just get yourself here and I'll have you decent."

"Shouldn't have bought Japanese, Abdool," Edith says as I skulk into the clinic. She heaves herself half out of her swivel chair and hurls a raincoat at me. Patients are always leaving behind umbrellas and jackets.

I keep my dissent oblique. "Short *u*," I correct. "Abdul. With a short *u*."

"Abdool." Edith is firm. "Rhymes with drool." She shakes open a stuck desk drawer and hands me a Hefty sack. "You Asians don't own the name. My sister just married an Abdool."

"How is Edna?" Annoying Edith isn't to my advantage.

"Shaquira," Edith mumbles without glancing at me. "Now she's Shaquira. You want to give me your things or what?"

The accident's left me oddly nostalgic for my first months in Oakland. I didn't co-own this building then; I leased clinic space from Fatty Ershad and had him shunt me patients he himself didn't want. Like Fatty, I was an ambitious transient. The motorized dental chair I've slumped into is the only souvenir of those live-cheap-and-get-rich-quick days. I'd bought this chair, together with a chair-mounted unit and light, through a classified ad. A widow already dreaming of cruises and casinos had priced it for quick sale. The widow had been chatty. "The profession's changed, you know," she'd cautioned. "Herb was depressed for years." Those days I lived for improving split-denture techniques. Now Herb's melancholy ghost menaces me with terrible times to come.

To scare the ghost away I scan the newest volume of the *Journal of Prosthetic Dentistry*. Colleagues, thank goodness, are still researching axis orientation transfer, still tracking muscle-function changes after orthognathic surgery, still perfecting partial glossectomy. They have so much to say about temporomandibular joints and maxillofacial prosthetics. Mrs. Herb, wherever you are, you were wrong. Herb changed, not our profession.

How far can a prosthodontist without clothes wander from his chair? Edith, who has a patient's perspective, calls this chair "the hot seat of suffering." To me it's the most relaxing piece of furniture I own to read in, so relaxing that, after the articles, I move on to Readers' Round Table, News and Notes, the Directory, until fine print swims. On the back cover, in an ad for a patent-pending resinous material, gum-pink dentures float like buoys in purple light that ripples like an ocean. I help myself to a box of Crayolas that some patient's child has left behind. The crayons doodle, delivering visions; my hand is only a medium. Mouth protectors and molars sprout all over the front cover. The molars metamorphose into cupids with Bibi-chaste faces, and wing their cheery way through Crayola lightning and rain to where, in place of colorless good sense, blood-red impetuous love prevails.

I am thinking how pleasant it is to laze in the dental chair instead of working on flawed mouths when a miracle—or catastrophe—happens. A woman I don't know, a beautiful woman with amber-dark skin, invades my clinic, perches herself beside me on this throne of suffering, and announces, "Doctor, you hurt."

Impetuous love needs no choreographing. Rubber-gloved fingers probe distresses, rapacious teeth shred inhibitions. I feel, by turn, virile, heedless, gallant. "My angel, my angel," I whisper. "Wicked, wicked boy," the invader laughs. We nibble and chew. Rosettes of blood decorate my face.

Then, as suddenly as it had begun, my adventure is over. We hear Edith's key in the front-door lock. The amber-skinned stranger wriggles back into clothes, socks, shoes, Frisbees a calling card at me, and rushes out.

QUAVONIA SMYTH

C.E.O., Dreams, Inc.
Elicitation & Facilitation
Special Events
Food Stylist

The phone on my desk rings and rings, a rebuke. It's a private line that patients have no access to. I entered this office a monogamous man.

"Abdool? You want me to get that?" Edith sounds breathless, a woman still sorting through her tote bag of lunchtime shopping.

I belt the borrowed raincoat over flagrant nakedness, float past bewildered Edith, who's holding out to me plastic-swathed pants, glide between closing elevator doors, stumble through a lobby full of patients in pain, and escape to the parking lot just as Quavonia, detective of unsavory desires, deliverer of delicious promiscuities, is starting up a pickup truck.

"Quavonia! Wait!"

The truck, flamingo-pink, whooshes out of the parking lot.

A peevish prosthodontist is, at heart, a flasher and felon. I borrow Fatty Ershad's Spiderveloce (he's shown me where he hides an extra key) and pursue Destiny's agent.

Sometime during the chase a muscled, brown-gold hand lunges out of the pink pickup, and a cake, a small two-tiered wedding cake, comes hurtling out. I brake into a whiplash-worthy stop, somersault into traffic, and, risking mutilation, sink to my knees before the wedding cake Quavonia's dropped.

It is the essence of cake: its Styrofoam skeleton pokes through pastel posies of marzipan.

A food stylist discards a prop after she has had it photographed. That shouldn't astonish; except that the bridegroom doll looks like me, has my bald, ovoid head, my bulging eyes, my slight paunch, my trim black goatee.

Yield. Succumb. Do It Today. I pluck the groom off his marzipan pedestal. A sign has been revealed. Rosettes stick to my cheeks. Styrofoam crumbles between my teeth. Icing coats my throat. On our wedding day in Sylhet, Fatima had fasted and I had picked at curried carp. Five hundred guests had ensured social approval. The priest had guaranteed a lifetime of virtue, peace, requital. A wedding cake is enticingly exotic.

I squat on the road. Cars swerve around me. I am a groom again, a greedy devourer of life's gifts.

A truck pulls up inches from me. I see pink fenders. The driver shouts down, "I see you got the cake."

From now on Destiny will smile.

Take Me as I Am

BRIAN KLAM

I turned up the driveway and could already see him out by the garage, him and his damn wrench bent over the tractor, right where I left him last week. He's a mechanical idiot, but he insists that piece of shit can be fixed, so let him try. I took my foot off the accelerator, so as not to violate his sacred speed limit, and coasted in beside one of the trucks. Okay, I said to myself, don't think, just go. Get it done. I breathed deep, then popped up and headed right for him.

"Before you say anything about this, you listen to me," I said, still ten feet away. "I give ten percent of my salary to charity. That's almost five thousand dollars a year. That's a lot more than you. And I work with underprivileged kids. I'm a good person. I only didn't tell you before 'cause I didn't want to hurt you. So before you say something stupid, think about that a second. Whatever you say is fine, it doesn't matter, I just wanted you to know, that's all."

My hand shot into the bowels of my purse and grabbed a pack of cigarettes and a lighter. I pulled the first puff deep into my lungs and stopped shaking. Looking up, I saw the trail of his smile hang and disappear. I had taken him completely by surprise. He looked awful.

Of course he hadn't washed this morning and sleep was hard and dried-up around his eyes, no matter that it disgusts us all and he knows it. Only after a minute did he break his stare and force it down into the tractor. His hands came alive again, fumbling with the wrench.

"Still seizing up?" I asked.

He muttered something and I said to check the oil, that the sediment builds up too fast. Last year it kept stalling, so I drilled a small hole in the carburetor, to give it air. I've always had a talent for machines—today I design stereo equipment for a major American manufacturer—but fixing that thing is beyond me.

He has two or three others that run perfectly well, but for some reason he keeps throwing money away on this one.

"It's just going to plague you. Junk it," I said. He looked up for a moment, but I don't think he saw me. Reflexively, I adjusted my dress, pulling the seams back to center.

He mumbled again, but his mouth was tight.

"I can't understand what you're saying," I said, blowing smoke towards the sky. I naturally tend to lose focus during stress and the physical action of smoking grounded me.

"Your mother—she got everything set up," he said. "Invitations is out—she's ordered this damn wedding cake—what's she supposed to do, throw it in the street?"

"What are you talking about?" I flicked the ash, then put the filter to my lips and inhaled. The wedding would be here, on my parents' ninety-eight-acre farm, in a week and a half. Georgette, my fiancée, adores the country, so this was the ideal setting. Behind the house, there's a thick lane of lush lawn. To one side is my mother's garden, a magnificent display of iris and peonies and other flowers, some bouncing in the breeze, some climbing an old wooden horse fence: faraway, if you squint, the garden looks like a patch of overgrown jelly beans. Fields and trees surround everything. Georgette and I were praying for blue skies, so the pictures would burst with color.

"It's a lot of trouble," my father said. "You put a burden on your mother. You should have told us sooner." He was talking into the tractor.

"I know it's a lot of trouble. I appreciate that," I said. "It's going to be a beautiful day. That's why I'm getting this over with now. I'm starting this new life, and I don't want anything holding me back." My voice cracked, so I stopped talking and smoked.

His head jerked up to argue, but once again my appearance caught him off guard. Finally, he choked out a whisper.

"What? Speak up, I can't hear you," I said.

"You didn't tell the girl? She don't know about all this?"

"She knows," I said. "Everybody knows but you. Now you know."

He couldn't take his eyes off the dress. It's a conservative pale yellow, hemmed just below the knees, with a nice high neckline. I bought it at Casual Corner, especially for this occasion, but years ago, when I first planned this. Also, no boysenberry lipstick, no false eyelashes. Just a little blush and a splash of Jean Naté. I even wore my breasts smaller today.

I tried to think of more to say, but got lost, basking in the liberation of the moment. I had been wearing dresses to work for a while now, and gaining a small measure of acceptance. This was the final step.

Just then, I realized my smoking was a secret, too. After one last drag, I flicked the butt down on the gravel and extinguished it with the point of my heel. I could see that the heels were a mistake. I'm tall anyway, but with these on I towered over him, a bigger-than-life version of his worst nightmare.

"Just apologize to your mother," he said. His voice was barely audible. "That's all I got to say to you."

"Mom knows. Everybody knows but you."

I stood tall, my nostrils flaring like Joan Crawford's in *The Women*. This moment had come so many times in my thoughts, it seemed now beyond my power, pulling me along, lifting the burden from me as I spoke.

He looked back down and let out a yell into the tractor. He had resigned himself to not being able to work on it, so he just held the wrench on this bolt and jiggled it.

"If you want to talk about this later, fine. I've got to make a call," I said, and tossed my curls. I turned to leave.

"You are not stepping in that house until you apologize to your mother."

I yelled, "You're as much to blame as I am!" He winced for who might hear.

"For crissakes." His voice was hushed. "Your damn cousins are driving from Canada, they probly left already. What the hell are we supposed to tell them when they get here?"

"I'm not telling them," I said. I thought, Why in the world tell distant cousins?

"They'll figure it out for damn sure when they get here," he said.

"What do you think? I won't be wearing the dress then! I'll be dressed the same as you! I'm wearing a tux. Is that what you thought? I'm not some kind of nut! My word! Georgette's wearing the wedding gown, and it's absolutely breathtaking: an off-the-shoulder lace bodice with details of taffeta, pearls, and rhinestones. A Nolan Miller original. We'll look just like any other couple."

I thought for sure that was what he was thinking, but then he looked confused or unsatisfied, as if I had answered the wrong question.

"You're getting married still?" he asked.

"Of course," I said. "I'm not gay."

"Oh," he said and stopped. "Oh." He scratched his cheek, then rubbed underneath his nose, wiping a gob of grease across his face like half a Fu Manchu mustache. His expression was thoughtful or vacant, looking out past me.

"I thought people like you moved to California," he said.

It might seem strange, but I was not at all prepared for my own father saying "people like you" to me. It meant I was no longer somebody like him. As obvious as it must appear, as striking as our differences are—me so tall, so finely groomed, him so squat and messy—and as effortlessly as I had discarded so many of his ideas and tastes, and as easily as I spoke against him, I always thought of myself as being quite like him. It's almost ridiculous, now that I consider it. But I would catch his face in my mirror and be stunned for a moment, and sometimes I would hear him in my voice. Georgette would often stop me and say, "I see him," or "I hear him," meaning my father in me, and we would laugh. I never thought consciously about it, but I liked that. I liked being like my dad. Deep down, past all our differences, I always thought we were a lot alike, me and my dad.

But now we saw each other so clearly in relation to the other, each separate and removed from the other: like we'd just noticed the other for the first time. He's so small, I thought, like a boy. His face wore that same blank confusion. I couldn't look away. We were quiet for a long time.

"The way you was talking, I thought you was saying goodbye."

"No," I said.

"Oh," he said. Something made a noise then. I think he dropped the wrench, but it sounded far away, like I didn't hear it, but only remembered it later.

"Well, why can't you wear that in private?" he asked. His voice was still quiet, but there was a hint of his normal, more accusatory tone, and it shocked me back to myself. "Why's this something you want to do in the open?"

"Because I'm not ashamed," I snapped, and walked away. I guess I shouldn't have hoped for understanding, and maybe it wasn't his fault, but that didn't mean I'd have to accept it. I got in my car. Coasting down the long driveway, I watched him in my rearview mirror, becoming smaller and smaller and smaller, until he might have been the candy groom on top of the wedding cake, an unflattering portrait of what I was soon to be.

Early Delivery

HANNAH WILSON

On Saturday nights she went out with Max because her friends had dates and she didn't want to stay home alone. Besides, he was okay—not pimply or grabby, and they liked the same kind of movies. Sometimes he borrowed his friend Tom's car. The lock on the trunk didn't work, so all the car's tools lay on the backseat. Spots of oil spread into a crazy-quilt pattern where a can of Quaker State had tipped over and leaked. She knew that one night he would have Tom's car and she wouldn't lie about her period. She was practicing how to ask whether he had a rubber.

The night it happened—a week after school let out and they each had their first summer paychecks—he borrowed the car and drove out along the Sound. The rayon blouse she had bought that noon clung to her sweaty body. He talked about his job. He thought his boss would let him move out of the warehouse soon into the shop, where he could start in assembly, and who knows? She didn't ask him who knows what, or anything else, even when he parked at the edge of a small city park away from the street-lights.

Afterward, he drove with one arm around her shoulder and talked some more about his job. She rolled her car window down all the way. They found an all-night place and stopped for a 3:00-A.M. breakfast. There were no towels in the bathroom, so she came out with her hands and face all wet, and when he saw her he started to lick off some drops. She pushed him away before the waitress came.

She ordered an omelet and hash browns and a short stack of blueberry pancakes. It all tasted of burned lard, but she was hungry and ate everything.

On the drive home she thought up the story she would tell her folks if they were awake—how they had picked up another couple, friends of Max's from work, how they had to wait for the second show because the line for the movie was so long. How everyone wanted something to eat after the show, but Max wouldn't take her into just any cheap diner so they drove a long way to a small café along the water. How Max had ordered a chocolate dessert, a soufflé the waiter called it, that the cook had to fix from scratch, and it took thirty minutes. They ate on a deck lit with Japanese lanterns, and where their reflections floated, the water turned to gold.

She prayed her folks would be asleep. Then she could take a hot shower. She felt sticky all over, and rumpled, especially along her neck and shoulders where Max kept stroking her. Her blouse would need three ironings. A hot bath would be better than a shower. She put her hand in his to get him to stop rubbing her, and he squeezed it and told her he had over four hundred dollars saved for the future. At a stoplight he bent over to kiss her, and she thought she ought to kiss him back. He said he could get the car next weekend.

When they reached the corner of 7th and Avenue M, the unmarked boundary between the city and her neighborhood, her insides deadened the way they did before she had to go into school or work on sunny days. The rows of closed doors on the small brick houses, the corner grocery, the playground across the street looked unfamiliar in the gray morning light.

Two blocks from home, they saw the Delite Bakery van parked in front of Chuck's Café, its back doors propped open. The driver was carrying a tray of bread into the coffee shop. When they caught sight of the wedding cake, Max slowed and then pulled to a stop right behind the open van. That close, they could see that the cake stood six layers high with sugar roses growing to the top. The bride and groom lay on their sides at the bottom of the tray. Maybe it's bad luck, she thought, to stand them side by side before the ceremony.

Max grinned at her and took out his pocket knife. He opened his door and motioned to her to get out too, but she sat still. Come on, he waved, and shaking her head no, she opened her door and got out. In a whisper, he bet her he could cut a slice of cake so the driver would never miss it. She wanted to shout NO, don't spoil their party, but the streets were so quiet she gave in to the hush. He cut a sliver from the side of the cake and held out half to her. She leaned forward to take it, afraid it would crumble through his fingers and mess the roses. She could feel it dissolving in her mouth when she got back into the car.

Dermot's Dream

JUDITH GUEST

Dermot O'Donnell, a fat, baldin' man of good stock and sweet temper, was an Irishman, not just by birth but by nature. That is to say, he believed in his dreams.

So it was on this bright mornin' he dragged out of bed, knowin' what he'd be seein' beneath his window even before he looked. And there it was; the weddin' cake in the middle o' the rhoad. Just as it had come to him in his dreams for three nights runnin': not fancy—no imps, nor swans holding up any carved pillars— just three small layers frosted in white, with pale pink rosebuds trailin' their pale green leaves.

Dermot stood in his boxer shorts, his heart a lump o' lead in his chest. He dreaded havin' to break the news to Charlie. Yet, how could he go up against his own histhry?

Dermot was the son of a Kerry sheep farmer, and at fourteen, he'd had a dream of a man dressed all in white perched high up in the branches of a tall trhee. He dreamt this for three nights, and on the fourth mornin', when he looked out his window to see the man smilin' and wavin' at him from his own beech trhee, he knew what it meant: he was to go to University and become a trhee surgeon. He'd thought to be walkin' down his own father's rhoad, but a callin' is a callin'. And it had worked out well for him. Until, some twenty years along in the trhee business, he'd had another dream—of a flower bed. Again, for three nights runnin' and the flower bed appearin' outside his window—green hostas, white tulips and arnge butterfly weed laid out like the flag of Ireland. The message was to become a travelin' landscape consultant for the Tidy Towns Competition. So he gave up his practice for a life on the road.

He had no permanent address. He made his home in the towns he'd helped to win the competition over the years. Sneem. Abbeyfeale. Ballybunnion. Athlone. Castlegregory. Cahirciveen.

And then on his sixty-seventh birthday, another drheam of three nights of the cave at the bottom of the cliff. 'Twas a somewhat more lithrary drheam. He knew it meant he was to settle down in the town o' Clifden, in the heart of the Connemara. Which he did, with no regrets. All the same, he'd been prayin' for no more messages, hopin' he'd used up his quota. Then had come the weddin' cake in the middle of the rhoad.

Over tea in Charlie's kitchen that afternoon, he took a gloomy bite of a bakewell tart. Charlie's blue eyes were fixed on him in sympathy. "You're sure it wasn't a birthday cake ye saw?"

"It had a little man in black on top, and a lady in a white lace drhess. I'm fated to travel fer the rest of me life, Charlie. I'm to be wedded to the rhoad. There can be no other meanin'."

Charlie lifted the pottery pitcher, tiltin' it toward his cup. "Will you be having milk with your tea?"

He shook his head. He drank his black, but it pleased him that she always asked, as though she didn't see him as a man with fixed habits. And her bakewell tarts were the best in the world, filled with her own strawbry jam, good enough to sweeten the sulkiest day. It was sad to think of teatime without them.

"This is the darkest hour o' me life." He had the Kerryman's way of overstatement.

"Ah, now, Dermot, let's think on this awhile. It mightn't be so grim as all that."

"You've been my best friend, Charlie. I hate to think of leavin' ya. Ya take care of me cat and bring in me mail. And you've a firm mind. It doesn't wander about like some strhay dog lookin' fer a trhee stump or a marrow bone, like mine."

"Me mind," Charlie said, "is noodlin' on something right now, Dermot. It's wonderin' who the lady is on top of the cake."

"The lady." Dermot went to the window, pushin' aside the lace curtains. Well. Learn slow, learn trhue. He turned round to see Charlie perched and smilin' at him in her sweet way. Across the room he came to take her in his arms. "Charlotte Duffy," Dermot said. "I just got the message."

The Subliminal Cakewalk Breakdown

AL YOUNG

Hey, great, I figured. Just aim the Toyota south, slap that stress-control tape into my cassette player, kick back behind the wheel, listen to the soothing New Age music, and let all those subliminal suggestions worm their way into my subconscious mind. Before I knew it, I'd be home and snug and tucked away from all the full-moon pandemonium going on around me.

As a matter of fact, even though the full moon was posited up there, beaming right down into my windshield as I roared off down the Nimitz Freeway, I was so deeply involved with my brand-new tape and with the quiet, subtle miracle it would be bringing about while I braked, steered, and sped up, that I didn't mind the heavier-than-usual traffic. It was really Wedge City out there.

To keep cool, I kept remembering what Irma Wong, the seminar's relaxation expert, had told us about slowing ourselves down. "Slow yourself down," she'd said in her talk. "Do that and observe how everything around you will instantly seem to slow down, too. We can't necessarily change conditions or circumstances whenever we wish, but we do at all times have control over how we react to what happens."

Okay, I was thinking, this is the worst Saturday traffic you've ever been in, but you don't have to take it personally, man. Just crank up the volume on that tape and concentrate on the road. One thing at a time, like Irma Wong says.

At first it seemed to be taking forever to get from one quarter-mile posting to the next. Before long, though, I wasn't paying attention to clock time at all. Now the music on that tape, the sounds of birds and ocean waves, all of which concealed subliminal suggestions, began to relax me. It felt good to know I was going to get my money's worth out of the investment.

When I started yawning, I thought: Uh-uh! Better be careful. Next thing you know, your arms are going to start getting heavy and your eyelids begin to droop. Then what? What if you do blank out right here on 880? What if you have an accident? What if you kill somebody? Or yourself? What if you crash into that mini-van of teenage girls just ahead of you, next lane over? Those girls are all your daughter Jodi's age. They don't deserve to die yet.

You yourself, well, you're middle-aged: you've done a lot. You've been married, had a kid, gotten divorced, done okay for yourself in Bay Area advertising, seen some of the world, and you might be marrying again. But, no, you want to see Jodi get through college and off to a solid start.

Whew! I was getting too worked up even to be out there on the freeway. It sure wasn't hard to see why everybody had been pushing me to attend Irma Wong's relaxation seminar. The business itself is stressful enough, and, being black, I'm much more subject to high blood pressure and heart disease than others.

Nikki Castle, my beautiful partner at the agency—and now my lover as well—had even gotten the seminar written into the budget of the account I was working on; the client would subsidize any relaxation research I did. After all, I was supposed to be writing convincing copy for an over-the-counter tension-relieving capsule. Even if I wasn't fond of the name, I had a job to do. Chill-Out. Is that offensive, or what?

"Stay in the moment; don't go getting ahead of yourself." The memory of Irma Wong telling us this in her soft, high voice was jolting. I tuned back in to the tape and the music and the sounds of the sea and sea gulls, and once I let go of my worries, I felt a lot better. But not for long.

By then traffic was rolling along at a nice clip. What made me nervous now was the realization that the car was gradually losing compression. Maybe I was imagining it; I couldn't tell. Slowly I pumped the gas pedal. Sure enough, the car didn't accelerate; it really was slowing down. First chance I got, I eased the Toyota over into the slow lane. That way, I figured, when all hell broke loose, I'd at least be able to coast onto the shoulder.

Slowly, though, I picked up an acrid, vaguely electrical smell that made me wonder if the car's wiring had either caught fire or short-circuited. You know what that's like. For all I knew, the car might even be ready to explode. Or was the smell even coming from my car?

The smell, it turned out, was coming from dozens of lighted emergency road fuses that flickered and sparked along the stretch in front of me. Cars were slowing, horns were blaring, and somewhere in the not-so-distant background I could hear sirens whooping and wailing.

There'd been an accident. No, actually, there'd been several accidents; the very kind of pileup I'd been envisioning a few miles back. As I poked my way around the scene of the catastrophe, I counted one-two-three-four-five cars that'd been crushed or dented or smashed.

Now I was antsier than ever. Danger still hung in the air; there were ambulances and highway patrol vehicles everywhere. I clicked on my signal to maneuver around a particularly pokey old Yugo. That's when I discovered that there was, indeed, something wrong with my electrical system; the battery was going out. I mashed my horn; it didn't sound. All the while, I was pushing down on the accelerator as hard as I could. The car would barely move forward. As I wondered what kinds of subliminal suggestions my trusty antistress cassette was feeding into my subconscious mind, I noticed how sweaty my face and underarms were getting.

Straining to stay calm, I reached again for the volume control on the cassette player, only to discover that the slowed, slurred tape was giving up the ghost altogether. Frightened, I snapped the damn thing off.

All-out panic had just kicked in when I observed that my headlights weren't functioning. Nor were any of my dash lights; I didn't have the slightest notion of how fast—or, rather, how slow—I was going. I bent to have a better look, but all I could see was how hopeless it was to stay on the road.

Rolling along, purely on what airline pilots call dead reckoning, I squinted through the dirty windshield at the freeway ahead. Over and over I asked myself: Where you gonna exit, man? It took a lot of looking to make out what I was seeing up the road, but it began to fall into place. There'd been some kind of rollover. Was it a van, a truck, a jeep, or what? Not that the type of vehicle mattered. My challenge was to maintain enough momentum to glide somehow around the wreck, then roll on off the scene at the very next exit.

Clinging to Irma Wong's inspiring talk, I gritted my teeth and said a prayer. If somehow I could make it down to that exit and into a service station for help, or else to a pay phone, I would never, *never* again let myself get caught on Highway 880 on a Saturday night, trying to haul ass from Oakland back home.

Of all the exits to come up, San Leandro was the one I was least familiar with. You'd think that after more than fifteen years of driving that stretch, zipping past it time and time again, I would know something about San Leandro. But I didn't. And when your car's gone dead and you're looking for a gas station, the last thing in the world you want to do is play a little game called Don't Get Lost.

Lost was what I was, however, and the only thing I had going for me was gravity. That is, the exit happened to be on a decline that carried me all the way down to a dark intersection. In no direction could I see anything that looked open. I rolled into what seemed like an industrial warehouse section of town. The Toyota was still on its roll, though, so I still had hope.

Another block and a quarter and everything changed. Suddenly I saw lights way down at the end of the street. Faint though they were, they were lights. Something was burning, something was open; somehow other human beings were involved. It wouldn't be long before I'd have to hop out of that car and start pushing like crazy. I hoped with my whole heart that we'd stay on a downhill course. I didn't want to believe what I thought as I got closer to those lights; I wasn't ready for any more accidents or emergency fuses.

When the car finally stopped short, shy of a truckstop driveway, I saw what it was that had been shining in the distance. Candles.

Yes, candles sticking up out of a cake as big as a fridge. From the way it was tiered and topped off with a sugary-looking likeness of a bride and groom, I figured it for a wedding cake. And right out there in the middle of the street!

What was going on here? I looked at all the big rigs parked around the shop and its airplane-hangar-sized garage. Then I read the battered metal sign: TOPPER'S TRUCK PIT.

When I slipped the car into neutral and got out to start pushing, I heard voices.

"Hold on there, pal, you need some help?"

"Yes," I shouted, startled.

Four men raced out of the darkness to push the car up the hump into the driveway.

"You hop in and steer," the oldest guy said. "We'll push it to the shed."

The shed where they had me park had dim lights the color of fluorescent bug lamps. And under the circumstances, my dress shirt and loosened tie weren't grimy or greasy enough. I felt foolish and too dignified. Every last one of the men who stood checking me out was white, and they all looked as if they'd been sent straight from Central Casting for a movie version of Buck Owens's hit record "Six Days on the Road," starring Willie Nelson.

"What's the matter with it?" the oldest fellow asked.

"All the power's gone out."

"Hmmmph," he grunted.

"You got a phone?" I asked.

"Well, the regular phone's locked up for the night. But there's a pay phone inside behind the cigarette machine."

"Hey, Bump," another fellow broke in, "don't forget Doyle will be calling in to let us know if he's bringing Margene over here for the celebration."

"Yeah," said the first man, facing me again. "Try not to tie up the line too long; it's the one we use for after-hours calls. You need change?"

"No," I said. "I got it covered."

"You belong to Triple A?"

"Yes."

"Well, I know the driver you'll be up dealing with, and it's Saturday night. He's all stacked up. They got him running around like a maniac."

I said, "If Triple A can't get me started, is there a good motel around here?"

All four truckers looked at one another, then sized me up again. One of them, a big, bearded joker, said to his big-bellied pal, "Hey, Panda, is he kidding? We don't know shit about motels around here, do we?"

After they'd all had a good laugh, Panda said, "What's your name, man?"

"Raymond," I told them.

"Well, Raymond," said the one who had the name Goodall sewn on his jacket, "why don't you pop the hood and let us have a look."

I said, "You guys gotta know all about this kinda stuff, right?"

"Wrong, wrong, wrong," said Goodall, "but pop the hood anyway."

"C'mon, Goody," said Panda, "let's see if we might can't help Raymond out."

"Dell," Goody said to the shortest man, a chunky smoker with long red hair curling out from under his baseball cap. The home-stitched logo above the cap's greasy bill proclaimed: SADDAM HUSSEIN GODDAM YOU'RE INSANE.

I popped the hood, and pretty soon all four of them—Panda, Goody, Dell, and a six-foot-fiver the others called Bump—were leaning over the engine with flashlights.

"I believe it's his brushes," said Dell. "They're probably out."

"Nope," said Bump, "it's his voltage regulator. When that thing goes out, you can get a hundred and twenty volts of household-strength current zapping your battery and frying your wiring."

Panda shone the flashlight down around the generator, then stepped back and cleared his throat. "Gentlemen," he announced, "don't overlook the possibility that it might be the man's armature that's give out."

"I'm going along with Dell," Goody said. "Nine times outta ten when this kinda thing happens, it's the carbon brushes. Had that happen with me up near Chico last week. And it's a pain in the ass, too."

"You can say that again," I said.

"Well," said Panda, "whyn't you go on back there and make your call to Triple A, while we fiddle around some more."

All this time, I'd had my back to the humongous wedding cake out there in the road. But when I turned to go inside Topper's Truck Pit, there it was again. If anything, the candles were brighter than ever.

I dug down into my money pocket. "Excuse me," I said. "I wonder . . . Could you tell me something?"

"What's that?"

"I don't think I've ever seen such a big cake all lit up. . . ."

Dell stomped out his cigarette and laughed. "Aw," he said, "that's a little surprise we got coming up for when the owner gets here."

"Someone getting married?" I asked.

"It's Topper's golden wedding anniversary," said Bump. "He and his wife'll be married fifty years today. If your marriage held that long, don't you think it'd be fun to have your pals pull something like this?"

"Topper's gonna out-and-out flip," Panda said. He looked at his watch. "Oughta been here by now."

"In fact," said Dell, "Topper shoulda been here more'n half an hour ago. Now that you mention it, if he don't get here soon, we're gonna be chowing down on candle wax."

After I had given the Triple A dispatcher the information she needed, I stepped back to admire a poster on the wall. It was for a new Bay Area soft drink our agency was handling. Castle & Sands might be having its problems, but we hadn't lost our touch. Looking at that beaming Polynesian woman in the midst of all those mouth-watering tropical fruits and palm leaves made me long to be on vacation. Even a micro-mini-vacation looked great. I couldn't wait till tomorrow, when my daughter Jodi would be joining me and Nikki. Already I could picture the three of us relaxing in the sun at Año Nuevo Beach.

When the pay phone rang, I picked up the receiver, ready to hear the operator tell me I hadn't dropped in enough coins to cover the call.

"Hello," I said warily.

"Topper's Truck Pit?" It was a deep but gentle male voice.

"Yes, it is."

"Who am I speaking to?"

"Oh," I said, surprised now and not thinking straight. "This is Ray Sands."

"Mr. Sands," the voice said. "This is the California Highway Patrol. There's been an accident."

My heart shot up into my throat. Images of Jodi and that vanload of girls I'd seen on the freeway crowded my mind.

"Is anyone hurt?"

"I'm afraid so . . . a Mr. Samuel Heard."

"Samuel Heard?"

"Yessir, Caucasian male, in his seventies. The address on his driver's license is the same as his business card—Topper's Truck Stop, right?"

"Yes," I said, relieved that no one I knew was being described. All the same, I was shaking. "Yes, this is the truck stop. Could you hold on, please?"

I left the receiver dangling and went back outside. Even though I didn't know Samuel Heard from Adam, I felt sorry for him.

"Panda, Bump, anybody," I said. "There's someone on the phone. One of you should talk with him."

"Who is it?" asked Bump.

"The CHP."

"What on earth do they want?"

"He says there's been an accident. Someone named Heard, Samuel Heard."

"That's Topper!" Dell yelled. "Something happen to Topper?"

"You'd better take the call," I said.

As Goody went off into the shop's dim innards, Panda, Bump, and Dell moved in close to where I stood and began asking questions.

"Is he alive?"

"Did they say how it happened?"

"Are they sure it's him?"

"Wonder if they called Margene?"

"Is that his wife?"

"Yes, the sweetest thing in the world. Now somebody's gotta call Doyle and tell him he won't have to pick up Margene."

"What about their kids?"

"What're we gonna do?"

"Oh, I hope he's alive."

Finally I said, "I'm sorry, I really am."

"Raymond, that's nice of you to say, especially since you don't even know the man."

"I feel like the longer I stick around here, the more I'm getting to know him."

"Topper was the greatest," said Goody. "We all loved him."

Panda, whose eyes were wet, got mad. "What're you talking like that for? Ain't nobody said anything about Topper being *dead*."

"I'm sorry," said Goody.

The craziness of it all must've gotten to me by then. I began to tremble, as much from exhaustion as anything else. I hoped nobody noticed. To steady myself, I leaned against the Toyota. My eyes hadn't been shut for more than a moment when I heard a commotion and there was a blue-and-yellow tow truck smoking up the driveway and headed straight towards us. Its front end was plastered with white frosting, chocolate crumbs, and smoldering candles; it was skidding on tracks of mushy wedding cake.

We all rushed and stumbled out of the way. The tow truck barely missed smashing into my dark car. Suddenly I heard other voices muttering as drivers—who'd been sleeping or napping—emerged from their rigs.

Goody was back, his eyes the size of silver dollars as he watched the five of us spreading out to avoid being hit by the tow truck gone haywire.

"Squelch!" he screamed. "What's going on? What the fuck is going on?"

Once he'd gotten himself collected and his truck hosed down, Squelch gave my battery a jump charge and told me, "What you need are new carbon brushes. The charge I gave you *should* hold up—long enough to get you to San Jose, if you don't stop. And don't play the radio or the stereo."

It was the longest thirty miles I've ever driven, and not only because I stayed in the slow lane all the way. To tell you the truth, I felt the oddest kind of exhilaration. Every moment meant something different from what it had before. I'd say it was because we found out Topper had survived that rollover. He had a minor concussion and had broken a couple of ribs, but he was going to be okay.

As for the wedding cake, the guys packed me up a huge chunk; enough for me to snack on, and still have plenty to share with Jodi and Nikki.

It occurred to me that whoever said that about not having your cake and eating it too might have got it all wrong. At the relaxation seminar, Irma Wong had told us we could have it all.

By the time I got to my home exit ramp, that full moon was sinking low and golden way over behind the mountains. It was such a restful sight. I knew that once I'd put the whole day in order, I would sleep the sleep of kings. It didn't even matter that I'd have to find a mechanic willing to work on Sunday.

Hat Trick

ALLEN WIER

The door opens into the windowless room, lets in the noise of rain splattering the street, light slanting across bottles and glasses. A man comes in wearing a long oilcloth slicker that slaps against his legs. He tips his head as if in momentary prayer and water runs off the wide brim of his hat.

Goddam Galveston weather, the man says to no one. Pouring down and the sun still shining. He pauses at a table by the door where a whore sits between two men, both her hands busy, one in each man's lap.

Devil's beatin' his wife, the whore says.

Water drips from the man's slicker and pools on the packed earthen floor; his boots are huge with mud. His left eye is fixed and unmoving, the other jumpy as a flea. A scar runs like a thin white mustache above his upper lip. He reaches beneath the slicker and a long-barreled military pistol clatters down onto the bar. His right hand rests on the pistol handle, his left hand beside it. Both hands are brown as the plank bar except for the darker whorl of a scar that looks like a knothole on the back of his left hand. The forefinger of that hand ends at the knuckle—his remaining fingertips are splayed, a curve of dirt black as pitch under each horn-thick nail. With a motion as natural as scratching an itch, the scarred hand reaches back down behind the bar and comes up with a full bottle of rum. The man bites hold of the cork with small yellow teeth and pulls the bottle off, spits the cork into a spittoon at his feet. With his fixed eye on nothing, he tilts the bottle and splatters the bar for the seconds it takes the barkeep to position an empty glass under the fall of rum. The man's fingers open to take the drink. His right hand has not moved from atop the pistol. He stoppers the bottle with the pink stub of his forefinger and tips glass and bottle back, downing the drink, spilling nothing.

The man smells like a wet dog. His name is Portis Goar, but he is called Eye. He's in Galveston to meet a shipload of German immigrants and lead them to one of Beale's Colonies. As usual, Eye's in the mud while someone else's in the money. Before the war, Eye worked a wrecker's boat scavenging the coast for shipwrecks from Galveston to Aransas Inlet. Threat of the Union blockade cut down on shipping, then a spell of calm weather cut down on storms, so he took a job of work as an enforcer for a broker in land grants. A dispute over property rights nearly cost him his life, but he only paid half a finger—his upper lip surprised him and grew back. After Texas seceded, he became a drover to avoid conscription. Texas beeves was drove to New Orleans to be shipped to hungry Confederate troops.

Now, Eye says, there is so many cattle over all of Texas, gone on the wild while the men was off fighting, they isn't worth more'n a dollar or two a head. You can have all the mavericks you can round up and brand, but at them prices, who cares.

It's a fact that money is a problem, the whore says.

Not havin' any makes me, Eye says, feel downright mean.

The whore looks up from her seat between the two men. Both her hands still moving, she asks, How mean?

Mean enough, Eye says.

Mean enough to do what he does.

The barkeep tops off Eye's drink.

You think red Indians is hard-assed, you ain't rode the immigrant trail. I have—the way I got this job. Took a steamer last fall thirty-six hours to the mouth of the Mississippi. At Pass à L'Outre a longboat ferried me off the steamer to the *Assurance* for her return voyage to Bremerhaven. That was bad enough, with just me and the crew and no shortage of supplies. But the ride on that immigrant ship was worse than bad dreams, and nightmares is the only way I'll ever ride a buckin' sea horse again.

The *Assurance*, a brigantine owned by Radeleff and Company, is an old tramp cargo ship, converted to haul immigrants. She was well-built but leaks a bit now. Solid, but slow.

Two masts, see—the foremast is square-rigged, and she's got a fore and aft mainsail with square maintopsails.

The whore rolls her eyes; she refuses to be impressed with this man's sailor lingo.

In Bremerhaven she had her anchor lines out for four days and nights, taking on stores and victuals. Four days Eye walked around that place and the sun never once come out. At least it's wet and green over there. On board, caulkers at work, smell of pitch and tar burns your eyes and nose, settles in your throat. Ship's carpenter replacing rotted boards near the stern. Stern end of the hold empty except for huge ballast stones and salt-shit-smelling bilge water that coats trousers black from the knees down. The carpenter's hammer echoes down in that wet dark emptiness. He stops hammering to wipe his cheek with his sleeve. Don't worry, he tells Eye, most of her is good oak, well seasoned. If she takes on water it's the caulkers coming up short. Then we'll join the poor settlers with a turn on the pumps.

Four days. Repairs complete. Revictualing complete. Immigrants show on covered riverboats from Bremen. Wooden crates packed with their necessaries are swung into the hold, aside the ship's store of salt pork, corned beef, peas, beans, rice, sauerkraut, potatoes, flour, and plums. Also, casks of drinking water, kegs of pickled herring for the seasickness, and a poke of doctorin' needs—quinine and Glauber's Salt.

May 8. Haul up anchor. Heave-ho. Hoist a sheet. Yessir, head 'em out. She rides low, heavy with the weight of so much longing, so much fear. Eye's slept on the desert and on the prairie, but at sea was the darkest nights he ever knowed. Down in them dark cabins, air stale and smelly around you, straw whispering tales ever' move you make, and under ever'thing, the roll and the sway to remind you how far you be from solid ground.

Babes cry. Men long for a shot of wine or a smoke, but wine is doled out small and no smokes allowed below deck. (Fires at sea—there's a hellish thought.) Peas and beans bloat up your stomach. Ever' other one gets the seasickness. Slop jars fill and spill. Men, women, and children lie in the smells their bodies make and pray for sleep. Water is short; nobody washes until it rains.

June 7. Boatswain's whistle—like some ole bird squawkin' out. Except for long lists of necessaries to bring over, the immigrant advice books start off in Texas. Don't mention storms that stir up the bottom of the ocean till the ship sails straight up and down. Strike topmasts. Can't know sky from sea—both gray-green, icy and salt-stinging, both howling mad. Sails down, but the wind's after the masts. Vomit, sea spray, and rain soak the upper deck. Not in them guide books is the look on Captain Henry's face, of purdee piss-your-pants terror.

June 12. Storm-battered. Repairs at sea. Not mentioned in the immigrant advice books, bilging—the godawful endless sound of water coming in through the hull; not mentioned is blood rushing to your brain and pounding with the pounding of the pumps, blisters on top of blisters from the pump handle, the fearful pumping of your heart and sucking of your lungs.

Eye breathes slow and deep, holds to the bar with his gun hand and empties his glass of rum.

June 14. Days off course after the storm. Low on drinking water, all portions halved. Not mentioned in the immigrant books are rancid pork, weevils in the flour, tongue-swelling thirst, and surly sailors.

June 16. The *Assurance* hails a five-masted clipper, the *Emma*, biggest immigrant ship afloat. She was out of Antwerp a full three weeks behind the *Assurance*. The *Emma* sends over one full barrel of water, half a keg of wine, a little corned beef, and enough bad news from Germany to worry all the settlers on the accounts of ones they left behind. Riots and maybe war behind them; the wide ocean and maybe Texas ahead.

July 6. The bilious fever—not mentioned in them books. Men, women, and children packed into little plank rooms in steerage. No portholes, just the spitting light of a whale-oil lamp, and air to breathe has to come down the stairs from the upper deck.

The fever-struck are stacked tight, four bunks on top of one another, locked in the smells of their own sweat and shit, them stinky sausages they brung, and the black vomit—not mentioned in no immigrant book. Some recover, plenty don't.

July 23. Five putrefying corpses sacked in sailcloth on the

foredeck, weighted at the feet with ballast rocks. A sailor called Little Joe holds the end of a board stuck out over the gunwale, a sixth body on that board, stuck out over the ocean. A face white as that winding cloth—a girl nineteen or twenty—sticks out of the burial bag. Her man bawls and holds the hand of a silent little girl, two or three. Captain Henry nods to a immigrant preacher who starts up a funeral song, *In dem Himmel ist's wunderschön*, about how wonderful heaven is . . . the husband gets to the rail and vomits overboard. Captain Henry stops the preacher quick. Captain Henry reaches into his coat and brings out a poke and tosses a fistful of tobacco over the body. Dust to dust. The quartermaster, Mr. Keene, brings out a big, curved needle and sews the bag closed. They lift the board with a hard jerk and the rocks inside slide, pulling the bag off and into the sea with hardly no splash. *Vater Unser*, Little Joe calls out, as if he were relaying an order from the mate. The little girl dabs at the vomit on her daddy's shirt. Little Joe and Mr. Keene are already lifting another body onto the plank.

Eye clinks his empty glass against the bottle and the barkeep pours him another.

August 7. North of Hispaniola. Watling's Island where Columbus landed, off to the northwest. Caulkers and pumps at work in the hold. Eye unties and reties knots up in the rigging on the mizzenmast to avoid a turn on the pumps, to avoid standing thigh-deep in choler and black bile—the humors of despair, to avoid breathing the foul-smelling darkness.

August 9. Becalmed on the tip of Haiti. Worse, even, than the unmentioned storms, seven days and nights of dead calm. The sea tightens like a corpse, the sky harder'n rock. A week of nights so dark and still you bite your arm to know you ain't already buried deep in your grave. Captain Henry drops a longboat to the island for firewood.

August 18. At anchor off the island of Cuba, loading the water barrels into a longboat. Not mentioned in them handbooks, how heavy the empty wooden barrels are, heavier still when the longboat returns. Not mentioned, clouds of mosquitoes. The men bring back a little coffee, plenty of sugarcane. The boatswain cuts a section of the cane and sucks the sweet juice, a stub of cane constantly in his mouth like some fat, green cigar.

August 19. A sudden wailing down in the hold. Frau Lindheimer delivers a smidge of a baby girl. Herr Lindheimer and Herr Schleuning take the first dipper of that Cuban water and name the baby . . .

Eye raises his glass in a toast.

. . . Johanna Galveston Lindheimer.

Eye turns the glass up and his Adam's apple bobs three times and the glass is empty again.

Some men of a *Gebirgssängerbund*, a singing society, sing songs. *Gott ist die Liebe*, about how loving God is, bless our children, keep us safe, bear us all to Texas. *Hin nach Texas!* Everyone sucks sticks of sugarcane. They talk about birds and flowers, they hug, they smile. Even that fellow whose woman got buried in the ocean, even he sings along. That was more'n Eye could take.

I took me a good stob and went down belowdecks to find me some rats to kill.

Eye holds out his glass and the barkeep fills it again.

Eye keeps wondering how bad can it be over there that they keep coming, full of questions as children. Load after load, he meets them at the dock with Mexican handcarts. They pile the carts high with trunks of Sunday clothes, as if there'll be anyplace fit to wear them, and farm tools, as if anything'd grow in the wild-horse desert he's leadin' them to.

They get a labor of land and a sixty-by-ninety-foot town lot—

a red square of dirt. Other colonies, Austin's, Dewitt's, Burnet's, give a league of land and two-acre town lot. Eye gets his pay all the same.

Eye turns and faces the whore, the shadow of his hat brim hides his expression, but she feels his jumpy eye moving all over her.

But I'm not so mean I don't hate my part. What's that fellow's expression in the book, *an exercise in futility.*

Sure, he tells them about the country. Land on fire. It burns. Wind rises with the sun and blows hot all day. Locusts buzz the noise of blood rushing in your ear. Land as far as you can see, red and crusty as a scab. Ever'thing that grows has thorns—mesquite, prickly pear, Spanish dagger. Ever'thing that breathes stings—ants, tarantulas, centipedes, scorpions, and snakes—ever' kinda snake from ever' kinda nightmare, 'cept there won't be no water moccasins like you seen near the Gulf. No more mosquitoes neither, 'cause there's not enough water. Prairie snakes fast as a horse at trot, rattlers slower and more deadly. Eye tells them all about it. It's a country of parasites you're walking a month to. Botflies lay eggs on horses, bore into stomachs and turn into worms. Gadflies lay eggs in old tick wounds and in a day and a half hatch maggots. What grows? Besides hardship and misery? Well, there's corn. You'll have cornbread for breakfast and coffee made from roasted corn; for lunch, corn mush with your cornbread; supper's the same, another cup of corn coffee, sometimes a jackrabbit all bone and muscle, sometimes prairie dog, and when you're hungry enough, prickly pear. Sure, you'll scatter them seeds you brung, you'll plant corn, melons, beans, peas—and ever'thing 'cept some of the corn will burn up and you'll wish it would too. Set out orange and apple trees, they wither and die.

He tells them, but you think it does any good? Listen, he tells them, cattle die of thirst. You'll share alkali water with your plow horse or mule till ever'thing burns up in the fields and you start thinking about horsemeat, mule steak.

The widow Krueger—Indians kilt her man, run off with her daughter, left her one son. Son went off his head in the heat, wandered around and fell into a den of rattlers coily as a nigger's hair. Eye was at the burying. Hot gust of wind come up and blew Widow Krueger's hat in the boy's grave. It plopped down on his blanket—no trees, no wood for a box. Now she goes hatless in the sun and hopes for her brains to fry.

Think on that, Eye says to nobody in particular.

But these people persist in their foolishness. The Lord's supposed to watch over idiots and children. Add immigrants. They cut loose the only nigger slaves in the colony. They make up to Meskins and talk about irrigation. Herr Lindheimer shoots a tough old deer and they invite the niggers and Meskins and a couple of starving old Indians. Thanksgiving—like them other pilgrims.

A crazy idea—coulda been anyone's, they all been too long in the sun—they gonna have a wedding party, marry ever' one to this new life. Eye reminds them married life's hell. No flour or sugar for a wedding cake, the women get three of their round hatboxes. Biggest box on bottom, middle-sized box next, then that air little one atop. For icing, they spread cornmeal mush over all and set him out in the sun to bake hard as adobe. Old man Waldeck produces a jar of powdered arsenic carried all the way from Germany to kill weeds and rats. Ain't no weeds and rats surviving here in the new land, so they put that poison to different use, mixing a spit-paste to whiten up the icing. Nobody better lick that bowl nor stick his finger in for a taste. Way they all waste most of the day on that cake, puts Eye in mind of them people in the Bible melting down that gold to make a cow idol.

Finally, a reason to open them trunks for fancy duds and keepsakes they toted across the ocean. Late afternoon and hot as the hinges of Hell; they set the wedding cake out in the dusty street and promenade in embroidered shirts with stand-up collars, wool frock coats, round felt hats that come outta them cake-shaped boxes. Their faces, red as the desert, stick out of white collars above black coats. They look like buzzards circling. Indians see that cake sitting out in the road, war dance all around it. Niggers laugh. Meskins call it a *fandango*.

Sun goes down sudden into the barren land, heat underfoot all night. Hot winds die down like a burned-out fire. Meskin guitars and Indian drums stir the still night air and it throbs with heat like coals.

All night they grin to beat the band, niggers and Meskins dancing and Indians doing pantomimes and ever' Dutchman singing a German beerhall song to the fiery taste of mescal.

Them people, they hang on to their foolishness like a comet to its tail. Eye shakes his head and polishes off the last dregs of rum in his glass.

And what for? Tomorrow, the wedding party's over and the sun hot as ever. No honeymoon out there. Next day, wool coats and felt hats packed back in trunks, put away with all their shivaree. Next day, that hollow wedding cake still be baking in the sun, so many layers of hot air, a graven image of sweetness poison to eat.

Their Wedding Journey

R. H. W. DILLARD

It seems that they have been traveling for days across this powdery expanse of smooth white snow, but Lorna knows that it cannot really have been that long, cannot have been very long at all. The country church where the wedding is to take place is, after all, only a couple of hours' drive from home.

It must be the silence, she thinks to herself, that is making time slow down or speed up or whatever it is doing. The road is unplowed, but the snow is so powdery that the tire sound of Syd's new radials is muffled completely. In the rearview mirror outside her breath-fogged window, she can see the clean arc of treadmarks stretching out behind them into the level distance.

Syd seems lost in thought, doing a deal or thinking about the bride's fresh young attendants whom he will hug and try to kiss with characteristic enthusiasm. Lorna has come to dread the occasional wedding to which they are invited, not because Syd makes a spectacle of himself—that he would never do—but simply because of that enthusiasm, that discreet expression of a dormant sexuality that she never sees at home in front of the children or recently even when they are alone or especially in bed.

The children are quiet, too. Tiffany and Michael began the trip noisily enough, poised in the backseat in their crisp clothes but soon quarreling and pinching each other, huddling to think up new ways to amuse themselves and annoy Lorna. Syd never seems to notice them at all unless at play one of them runs loudly into him or breaks something in the house that he has defined as his. But now they are quiet, too, staring out at the snowscape, their breathing as steady and quiet as if they are in a trance or a dream.

Lorna, tired of their squealing and giggling, had set them to counting things, cows in fields, bunched together against the winter wind, or dark birds on the power lines, or trees with their leaves still on in the bare, snowy fields. But not long after Lorna woke up from her nap or dizzy spell or simple lapse into automotive reverie, Tiffany complained that there was nothing left to count, and all Lorna could see when she looked was a snowy smoothness and distant irregular crenellations of hillocks and bushes buried in ice and snow. But before she could think of another game to entertain and quieten the children, they had lapsed into a stillness as profound as the silence in the snowy fields around them.

The insidious warmth of the car heater and the steadiness of Syd's driving make Lorna drowsy again. She wipes at the steamy window beside her with a tiny embroidered handkerchief, careful not to smear the glass with her bare hand and incur a sarcastic comment from Syd. She can barely make out the distant, steep flank of a white mountain before the glass steams over again, and for the briefest of seconds, she thinks she sees high, high atop the tiered white precipice two distant, gigantic figures, side by side. Like a bride and a groom, she thinks, as if some local Ikhnaton had decided to erect on the nearest mountaintop a vast monument to the perfection of his marriage to an unchangingly beautiful and perpetually sensitive and loving Nefertiti. I must already be dreaming, she thinks, as with a slight jerk and a contented sigh she does drift into an unclouded sleep.

Syd is not thinking of the bridesmaids he will see and meet at the wedding reception later this afternoon. He does always enjoy kissing the flushed faces of eager brides, and he does enjoy looking at and maybe even teasing and touching the clusters of brightly colored maidens who stand in lively prelude to the bride in the receiving lines. But he knows that if he does start thinking about them now, of young women sprawled easily over armchairs, bare lithe legs dangling appealingly from articulate knees just edging out from under skirt hems, or young women in crinkling bright gowns all in a row, their smooth small breasts tantalizingly veiled as they nod and bow in the stir of passing guests, knows that if he does start thinking about them now Dr. Dick might stir and shift in his trousers and Lorna, who never misses a thing that he ever wants her to miss, would notice for sure and as surely misunderstand.

He drives at a steady rate through the powdery icing of the snow, the road almost obscured but steadily arcing to the right around the flank of the mountain. He does not want to doze off or feel dizzy the way he did a few miles back, not even for a second, so he begins to think methodically of marriage in general, and of his marriage to Lorna in particular.

He remembers how desperately in love and how clumsily lustful they had been on their honeymoon, how after the bellhop had gone away into the Niagara night, they had gone back out into the hall and he had attempted to carry Lorna over the threshold into their rented room. They had been giggling furiously and were nervous about being observed, and Syd had started forward before he had Lorna completely lifted in his arms. As she had shifted and attempted to balance herself, he had tripped over his own foot and pitched forward into the doorframe, spilling Lorna onto the thick pink rug of the floor and splitting his right front tooth off practically at the root.

Syd stirs nervously in the car seat as he remembers the sharpness of the blow and the terrible finality of seeing his own tooth lying in his palm after they had crawled around on the rug until they found it under the tip of the heart-shaped bed. There had been no blood and, oddly enough, no pain; only a jagged stump whose contours felt to Syd's obsessively probing tongue exactly like the shape of the abandoned rock quarry where he and Lorna had only the summer before fumbled and thrust their way out of frustrated innocence and ultimately into wedlock.

A funny thing, Syd thinks as he has so often thought before, the effect that broken tooth has had on my life. His thoughts move back again to his and Lorna's honeymoon, how they had stopped crying and laughing at the broken tooth, how Lorna had put it in her purse along with their traveler's checks and the Xerox copy of their marriage license "just in case," and how they had rushed each other's clothes off and climbed onto the satiny slick red heart of the bed and begun to make love. Syd feels Dr. Dick stir as he remembers, but there is no holding back now as his memories rush over the precipice of his defenses like raging Niagara that night.

They had made love five, six, maybe even seven times that night, and always as they had rushed toward climax together his tongue had raked itself raw on the ragged contours of the stub of his tooth. The next morning, dim and damp, the falls rumbling beyond the restaurant window, his tender tongue had plowed its way through the mushed eggs and bacon in his mouth to find the gap of the tooth, and he had had to rush Lorna back to their room, doubled over and feigning a stomachache to conceal his passion, and they had done it again and again all that gray day, Lorna once running her long tongue into his mouth and pushing his own tongue away from the tooth until she bucked and winged her way into an orgasm more powerful than any that had preceded it.

Dr. Dick is bent and shoving hard against Syd's fly as he glances guiltily to his right at Lorna, but her head has lolled against the window as she is apparently dreaming, her eyelids fluttering and her lips parted slightly.

Syd forces himself to think of his many trips to the dentist, of the needles and drilling, of the looming root-canal specialist whose breath had been as foul as the tomb, so terrible that Syd had gagged and nearly choked right in the examination chair, of the curved apparatus filled with pink putty that had been forced up onto his gums, and finally of the shining and perfect new tooth that had been screwed into place in his mouth. As Syd goes over the terrible experience, Dr. Dick begins to subside and just in time, as Lorna is stirring and sitting up.

Syd has no idea how long she has been asleep or exactly how far they have traveled while he has been thinking, but he does allow himself one more thought before settling back into the tasks of his driving. He thinks how since that tooth was repaired, he has never truly enjoyed sex with Lorna, not even the nights when he sired Tiffany and Michael. He thinks, with some confusion and a great deal of wonder, how just when he achieves penetration, his tongue always seeks out the tooth and how when it finds the smooth German porcelain of his expensive crown all his pleasure seems to slide away on that perfect surface. I always complete my task, he thinks to himself, but I never enjoy it. And suddenly he feels empty and afraid and completely alone, as though Lorna and Tiffany and Michael were as unreal as their unnatural silence and as empty of meaning as the white untraveled road that stretches mindlessly before him, so he shuts off his troubling thoughts as completely as if they were just another gadget on the car which could be switched off with a mere flick of the driver's wrist.

Lorna has been dreaming of the giant figures she thought she saw through the fog on the window on the mountaintop.

She has always been a fan of gigantic statues. She had wanted to go to Mount Rushmore on their honeymoon, but Syd had insisted on a traditional wedding journey to Niagara. She has always felt that Syd would never have broken his tooth and brought them endless bad luck by dropping her on the threshold of their marriage if only they had been protected by those massive carved guardians in South Dakota. She buys and keeps every magazine she sees that features huge statuary on the cover: a *National Geographic* with the Sphinx dreaming in the desert or a cracked Olmec head tilted in the jungle; a *Newsweek* with stony Ferdinand Marcos staring unfinished at a land in turmoil, or a science fiction magazine with tiny awed explorers staring up at an overwhelming alien visage looming over a purple plain. She insisted that they buy a VCR, ostensibly so that Tiffany and Michael could take advantage of educational tapes, but really so that she could purchase her own copy of *North by Northwest* and visit the Mount Rushmore of her desires with Cary Grant over and over again.

So it comes really as no surprise to her that she has been

dreaming of two enormous statues of a bride and groom poised high above her, and that in the dream she floated right up to them and hovered like a bird or mundane helicopter before their huge, placid faces: the bride's, veiled and distant and calm; the groom's, showing no emotion at all, staring straight ahead, the lips tight over his doubtless perfect teeth.

The dream had no plot or even any distinct end. The only thing she is sure of is that it was completely unlike her earlier dream—or swoon—before the car and the snowy world became so silent. No, this was just a dream, a lovely dream with no unsettling qualities or even a hint of strangeness, just beauty and wedding wonder.

She looks at imperturbable Syd staring ahead at the white unmarked road and, over her shoulder, back at the two silent children, so clean and still, so distant in their own worlds in the backseat. It is almost as if she does not know them, her own babies, so far away they seem.

She thinks back to that moment of giddiness or brief slumber before she became so estranged from her surroundings. What a unique and special moment, she thinks, but one that seems strangely familiar. I can almost imagine what I looked like as it happened, she thinks, as though my amazed face were huge and perfectly carved in lasting stone, that dizzy moment held for the contemplation and awe of centuries to come. I must still be asleep, she thinks, if I am capable of such thoughts, and she shakes her head and begins examining her dress to make sure she hasn't mussed it in her sleep, for surely they must be nearly there.

And then, as bright and fresh as though it were happening at that exact second, Lorna suddenly remembers when she has had a strange experience like that before, remembers it precisely and exactly.

She and Syd were already in their traveling clothes, their wedding clothes safely in her mother's care, Syd's cutaway to be
returned to the rental store and her white dress to be folded and
pressed with sachets in crinkling white paper and reverently in-
terred in a brassbound trunk in her mother's attic. They were
standing together behind the wedding cake, facing a roomful of
laughing friends and relatives and absolute strangers invited by
their respective parents. They were holding a gleaming knife over
the white three-tiered wedding cake, smooth and white and en-
crusted with sugary white decorations, doves and bells and looping
wreaths of white roses. They were smiling and holding the long
sharp knife over the surface of the cake while cameras flashed
and clicked and whirred around the room.

It was then, just then, that Lorna felt the room blur for a
second, felt her head spin, looked down at the surface of the cake
as though to steady herself visually, since she could not release
her grip on the knife to put her hands down. And she was sure
that she saw, just then, at that moment, a road in the middle of
the wedding cake and a tiny car plowing its steady way across the
powdery icing and even, she must have imagined, four tiny figures sitting silently in the tiny car. And just as she began to lean
down for a closer look, she felt Syd's hand moving the blade of
the knife down, and together their hands sped it down and into
the cake and through the car and into her reverie. Everyone was
cheering and laughing as the flashes split the room. And then
everything was all right, and it was her wedding day, and she
was pressing a large, uneven piece of crumbly white wedding
cake into Syd's laughing mouth, smooshing it into his gleaming
teeth, and she never thought again of that momentarily unsettling
vision until this moment.

Lorna gasps and looks at Syd. He does not notice, is peering
carefully through the windshield at the road ahead, at their un-

faltering progress across the empty landscape. The children are still silent, and the flat world around them still and unchanging. Lorna is almost frightened, but she notices, stretching ahead of them on the familiar surface of the road, that now a single pair of tire tracks is preceding them, leading them toward the pleasures of the wedding before them. She feels a sudden warmth, a great and unyielding affection for Syd, as though something has come full circle, a longing for him such as she has not felt for years, perhaps not since those delirious first days of their honeymoon. She glances around quickly at the children, who are both staring out of the windows at the monotonous snowy landscape, before she reaches her hand over to Syd's thigh, feels the muscular tension of his foot's steady pressure on the accelerator pedal through her fingers. She wants to speak to him, to say something that she has never said to him or to any living person before, but the silence of the car holds her in her own silence. She squeezes his leg, and just as Syd's startled face begins to turn toward her, she feels suddenly dizzy again, as though she were lifting out of her body and settling quickly back into it again.

Lorna senses Syd looking directly at her, feels his muscles tighten as he touches the brake and starts to slow the car in the treacherous snow. She senses that Tiffany and Michael are straightening up in the backseat, beginning to lean forward toward her. She has a sudden sense of terrible loss. Her eyes are a flutter of darting lights, the whole landscape seems to be flickering and shimmering as high above the car something huge flashes once and begins a terrible descent.

Syd and Lorna react to the burst of applause that greets their cutting of the cake by smiling, giving each other yet another kiss, and raising the clotted cake knife aloft in triumph. Lorna is blushing now after a brief moment of shy paleness. As they prepare to make the second cut amid the chatter of cameras and the hooting of friends, Syd allows his eyes to pass down the row of bridesmaids, each at that moment prettier than the other, but Lorna looks only up at Syd. She squeezes his hand, and he turns his dazzling smile directly and only to her, but Lorna looks through and past the perfection of Syd's smile, past the room full of friends and well-wishers, past this singular moment in time to where the future stretches out before them like a smooth white road curving indefinitely into unending days of delight.

Contributors' Notes

RICHARD BAUSCH
Twice a finalist for the PEN/Faulkner Award, Richard Bausch
is the author of five novels—*Real Presence, Take Me Back, The
Last Good Time, Mr. Field's Daughter,* and *Violence.* His two
collections of short stories are *Spirits* and *The Fireman's Wife.*
He teaches at George Mason University and lives with his wife,
Karen, and five children in Broad Run, Virginia.

CHARLES BAXTER
Charles Baxter lives in Ann Arbor and teaches at the University
of Michigan. He is the author of the much-praised novel *First
Light,* and three collections of stories, *Harmony of the World,
Through the Safety Net,* and, most recently, *A Relative Stranger.*
His stories have been selected for *Best American Short Stories,*

the O. Henry prize collection, and numerous other anthologies. He has also published a volume of poetry, *Imaginary Paintings*.

ANN BEATTIE
Born in Washington, D.C., and educated at American University and the University of Connecticut, Ann Beattie now divides her time between Charlottesville, Virginia, and York, Maine. She is married to the painter Lincoln Perry. Her collections of stories include *Distortions, The Burning House, Secrets and Surprises,* and *Where You'll Find Me.* Her novels are *Chilly Scenes of Winter, Falling in Place, Love Always,* and *Picturing Will.* Her latest is a collection of stories—*What Was Mine.*

MADISON SMARTT BELL
Madison Smartt Bell comes from Nashville, Tennessee. He studied at Princeton (B.A.) and Hollins College (M.A.). He lived and worked in New York City as a security guard for Unique Clothing Warehouse and as a sound man for Radio-televisione Italiana. Born in 1957, he is the author of six novels—*The Washington Square Ensemble, Waiting for the End of the World, Straight Cut, The Year of Silence, Soldier's Joy,* and *Doctor Sleep.* He has also brought out two collections of his short stories— *Zero D/b* and *Barking Man.* Bell is an outstanding banjo player and has taught Asiatic martial arts professionally.

RON CARLSON
Born in Logan, Utah, Ron Carlson studied at the University of Utah and then from 1971 to 1981 taught at Hotchkiss School in Connecticut before returning to write in the West. He now lives in Tempe, Arizona, and teaches at Arizona State. His books include the novels *Betrayed by F. Scott Fitzgerald* and *Truants*

and the highly praised collection of short stories *The News of the World.*

KELLY CHERRY

Now Professor of English at the University of Wisconsin–Madison, Kelly Cherry was born and grew up in Richmond, Virginia. She was educated at Mary Washington, the University of Virginia, and the University of North Carolina at Greensboro. Her novels are *Sick and Full of Burning, Augusta Played, The Lost Traveller's Dream, In the Wink of an Eye,* and *My Life and Dr. Joyce Brothers: A Novel in Stories.* An essayist and a poet as well as a fiction writer, she received the first Poetry Award given by the Fellowship of Southern Writers in 1989. Her most recent book is *The Exiled Heart: A Meditative Autobiography.*

R. H. W. DILLARD

Longtime director of the highly regarded creative writing program at Hollins College, R.H.W. Dillard is the author of four books of poetry and has published or edited several critical works and anthologies. His novels are *The Book of Changes* and *The First Man on the Sun.* He was coauthor of the film *Frankenstein Meets the Space Monster.*

STUART DYBEK

Born and raised in Chicago, poet and story writer Stuart Dybek lives in Kalamazoo and teaches at Western Michigan University. He is the author of a book of poems, *Brass Knuckles,* and of two collections of short fiction: *Childhood and Other Neighborhoods* and, most recently, *The Coast of Chicago.* Dybek's stories have been chosen for the O. Henry Prize story collections and *Sudden Fiction International,* and he has received a Whiting Writers Award.

GEORGE GARRETT

George Garrett is a teacher and writer who lives in Charlottesville, Virginia, and works at the University of Virginia. He is the author of twenty-four books, including novels, short stories, poetry, plays, and a biography of James Jones. He is editor or coeditor of nineteen other works, including this one. In 1990 he was the recipient of the PEN Malamud Award for Excellence in the Art of the Short Story.

MARITA GOLDEN

Marita Golden's autobiography, *Migrations of the Heart,* and her novels, *A Woman's Place* and most recently *Long Distance Life,* which follows the life of an African-American family in Washington, D.C., from the 1920s to the present, have received an outstanding critical reception. Born and raised in Washington, she did her undergraduate work at American University and her graduate work, in journalism, at Columbia University. She has written for a wide variety of publications and has worked in television. She taught for three years at the University of Lagos in Nigeria. Ms. Golden has also written and published poetry, and her poems have been included in a number of anthologies.

BEVERLY GOODRUM

Beverly Goodrum grew up in Charlotte, North Carolina. She has attended the University of North Carolina–Chapel Hill (B.A.), Yale University (M.A.), and the University of Virginia (M.F.A.). Her stories have appeared in a number of little magazines, and she was the winner of The Writer's Eye Prize for 1989. She has taught at Virginia Commonwealth University, the University of Richmond, and the University of Virginia.

JUDITH GUEST

Ordinary People, Judith Guest's first novel and the first unsolicited manuscript accepted by Viking in twenty-six years, became a startling success, first as a best-selling book in both hard cover and paperback, then as a film by Paramount. Her next novel, *Second Heaven,* was a Book-of-the-Month Club selection. Born in Detroit, she went to the University of Michigan and, for a time, taught public school in Michigan at Royal Oak, Birmingham, and Troy. She is the mother of three sons. With Rebecca Hill, Guest coauthored *Killing Time in St. Cloud* (1988).

PAM HOUSTON

Pam Houston lives in Park City, Utah. Her first collection of stories, *Cowboys Are My Weakness,* was published by Norton in 1992. Her stories have appeared in *Mademoiselle* and *Mirabella,* and one was selected for *Best American Short Stories, 1990* (Richard Ford, Guest Editor). She is a Ph.D candidate at the University of Utah, and is managing editor of *Western Humanities Review.*

JOSEPHINE HUMPHREYS

Dreams of Sleep by Josephine Humphreys won the Ernest Hemingway Award for a first work of fiction. Since then she has written and published *Rich in Love* and *The Fireman's Fair.* A native of Charleston, South Carolina, she attended Duke University, where she studied writing with William Blackburn and Reynolds Price. She lives in Charleston with her husband and two sons in a classic antebellum house on Society Street.

BRIAN KLAM

A former student of Madison Smartt Bell, Brian Klam was educated at the University of Maryland and Hollins College. Except for a period of time spent in Japan, he has lived mostly in Baltimore. He has worked as a writer for advertising agencies. "Take Me as I Am" is his first published story.

DAVID LEAVITT

Family Dancing, David Leavitt's first collection of stories, was a finalist for both the PEN/Faulkner Prize and the National Book Critics Circle Award. His most recent collection is *A Place I've Never Been*. He has also published two novels—*Equal Affections* and *The Lost Language of Cranes*. Awarded a Guggenheim Fellowship in 1989, he lives and writes in East Hampton, New York.

GREGORY MCDONALD

A Harvard man (class of '58), Gregory Mcdonald is probably best known for his highly successful detective novels, particularly the Fletch series, which began in 1974 with *Fletch*. He served in the Peace Corps in its early days and from 1964 to 1973 was editor of arts and humanities for the *Boston Globe*. Writing full-time since then, he has produced, among other books, nine Fletch novels, three Flynn novels, and the first two novels, *A World Too Wide* and *Exits and Entrances*, of a quartet entitled *Time*. These days Mcdonald lives and works on a large old farm near Pulaski, Tennessee.

BHARATI MUKHERJEE

Born and raised in Calcutta, Bharati Mukherjee first came to the United States in 1961 and has been a permanent resident since 1980. She received her M.F.A. and Ph.D. degrees from the University of Iowa. Beginning with her first novel, *The Tiger's Daughter*, she has continued to produce both fiction and non-fiction and received widespread recognition for *Jasmine*, which was nominated for the *Los Angeles Times* Book Award in fiction.

Her book *Middleman and Other Stories* won the National Book Critics Circle Award. She has taught at a variety of places— Marquette University, the University of Wisconsin, Montreal University, Skidmore College, the University of Iowa—and now lives and works in San Francisco.

MARY LEE SETTLE

Mary Lee Settle's first novel, *The Love Eaters*, was published in 1954. Since then she has brought out twelve novels, most recently *Charley Bland*, and four nonfiction books. At this writing she has a new novel in process and has just published a travel book—*Turkish Reflections: A Biography of a Place*. She is best known for the extraordinary five novels which form *The Beulah Quintet*, covering a span of time from the age of Cromwell to the present. She has taught at Bard College and the University of Virginia and now lives with her husband, journalist William Tazewell, in Ivy, Virginia.

ALLEN WIER

Allen Wier comes from Blanco, Texas, and teaches at the University of Alabama. He is the author of three novels—*Blanco*, *Departing as Air*, and *A Place for Outlaws*. He has also published *Things About to Disappear*, a widely praised collection of short stories. Wier has received a Guggenheim Fellowship and a National Endowment for the Arts grant. He and his wife and son live in Tuscaloosa.

JOY WILLIAMS

Joy Williams is the author of the novels *State of Grace*, *The Changeling*, and *Breaking and Entering* and of the story collections *Taking Care* and *Escapes*. She has also written *The Florida Keys: A History of Key West*, with her husband, the writer and editor Rust Hills. Her honors include a National Endowment for the Arts grant, a Guggenheim Fellowship, and an Award in Literature from the American Academy and Institute of Arts and Letters.

HANNAH WILSON
Hannah Wilson was a summer writer for the twenty-two years that she taught high school English in Istanbul, in Ibadan, and in Eugene, Oregon, where she retired and now lives and writes full-time. Her poems have appeared in *Calyx* and *Fireweed*. "Early Delivery" is her first nationally published fiction.

AL YOUNG
A native of Ocean Springs, Mississippi, Al Young has lived since 1961 in the San Francisco Bay Area. He is the author of five novels, including, most recently, *Seduction by Light*, six collections of poems, and two books of essays. He has also written screenplays for Sidney Poitier, Bill Cosby, and Richard Pryor. Young has received a Guggenheim Fellowship and a National Endowment for the Arts grant and has been a Fulbright Fellow in Yugoslavia.